Malaeska

Ann S. Stephens

ISBN. 197641797X

ISBN-13: 978-1976417979

Table of Contents

CHAPTER I.

The brake hung low on the rifted rock With sweet and holy dread, The wild-flowers trembled to the shock Of the red man's stealthy tread; And all around fell a fitful gleam Through the light and quivering spray. While the noise of a restless mountain-stream Rush'd out on the stilly day.

The traveler who has stopped at Catskill, on his way up the Hudson, will remember that a creek of no insignificant breadth washes one side of the village, and that a heavy stone dwelling stands a little up from the water on a point of verdant meadow-land, which forms a lip of the stream, where it empties into the more majestic river. This farm-house is the only object that breaks the green and luxuriant beauty of the point, on that side, and its quiet and entire loneliness contrasts pleasantly with the bustling and crowded little village on the opposite body of land. There is much to attract attention to that dwelling. Besides occupying one of the most lovely sites on the river, it is remarkable for an appearance of old-fashioned comfort at variance with the pillared houses and rustic cottages which meet the eye everywhere on the banks of the Hudson. There are no flowers to fling fragrance about it, and but little of embellishment is manifest in its grounds; but it is surrounded by an abundance of thrifty fruit-trees; an extensive orchard sheds its rich foliage to the sunshine on the bank, and the sward is thick and heavy which slopes greenly from the front door down to the river's brink.

The interior of the house retains an air of substantial comfort which answers well to the promise conveyed without. The heavy furniture has grown old with its occupants; rich it has been in its time, and now it possesses the rare quality of fitness, and of being in harmony with surrounding things. Every thing about that house is in perfect keeping with the character and appearance of its owner. The occupant himself, is a fine stately farmer of the old class—shrewd, penetrating, and intelligent—one of those men who contrive to keep the heart green when the frost of age is chilling the blood and whitening upon the brow. He has already numbered more than the threescore years and ten allotted to man. His habits and the fashion of his attire are those of fifty years ago. He still clings to huge wood-fires, apples, and cider in the winter season, and allows a bevy of fine cows to pasture on the rich grass in front of his dwelling in the summer. All the hospitable feeling of former years remains warm at his heart. He is indeed a fine specimen of the staunch old republican farmer of the last century, occupying the house which his father erected, and enjoying a fresh old age beneath the roof tree which shadowed his infancy.

During a sojourn in this vicinity last season, it was one of our greatest pleasures to spend an evening with the old gentleman, listening to legends of the Indians, reminiscences of the Revolution, and pithy remarks on the present age, with which he loved to entertain us, while we occasionally interrupted him by comparing knitting-work with the kind old lady, his wife, or by the praises of a sweet little grandchild, who would cling about his knees and play with the silver buckles on his shoes as he talked. That tall, stately old man, and the sweet child made a beautiful picture of "age at play with infancy," when the fire-light flickered over them, to the ancient family pictures, painted in Holland, hanging on the wall behind us, in the old-fashioned oval frames, which, with the heavy Dutch Bible, which lay on the stand, secured with hasps and brass hinges, ponderous as the fastenings of a prison-door, were family relics precious to the old gentleman from antiquity and association. Yes, the picture was pleasant to look upon; but there was pleasure in listening to his legends and stories. If the one here related is not exactly as he told it, he will not fail to recognize the beautiful young Indian girl, whom he described to us, in the character of Malaeska.

3

At the time of our story, the beautiful expanse of country which stretches from the foot of the Catskill mountains to the Hudson was one dense wilderness. The noble stream glided on in the solemn stillness of nature, shadowed with trees that had battled with storms for centuries, its surface as yet unbroken, save by the light prow of the Indian's canoe. The lofty rampart of mountains frowned against the sky as they do now, but rendered more gloomy by the thick growth of timber which clothed them at the base; they loomed up from the dense sea of foliage like the outposts of a darker world. Of all the cultivated acres which at the present day sustain thousands with their products, one little clearing alone smiled up from the heart of the wilderness. A few hundred acres had been cleared by a hardy band of settlers, and a cluster of log-houses was erected in the heart of the little valley which now contains Catskill village. Although in the neighborhood of a savage Indian tribe, the little band of pioneers remained unmolested in their humble occupations, gradually clearing the land around their settlement, and sustaining their families on the game which was found in abundance in the mountains. They held little intercourse with the Indians, but hitherto no act of hostility on either side had aroused discontent between the settlers and the savages.

It was early in May, about a year after the first settlement of the whites, when some six or eight of the stoutest men started for the woods in search of game. A bear had been seen on the brink of the clearing at break of day, and while the greater number struck off in search of more humble game, three of the most resolute followed his trail, which led to the mountains.

The foremost of the three hunters was an Englishman of about forty, habited in a threadbare suit of blue broadcloth, with drab gaiters buttoned up to his knees, and a hat sadly shorn of its original nap. His hunting apparatus bespoke the peculiar care which all of his country so abundantly bestow on their implements of sport. The other two were much younger, and dressed in home-made cloth, over which were loose frocks manufactured from the refuse flax or swingled tow. Both were handsome, but different in the cast of their features. The character of the first might be read in his gay air and springy step, as he followed close to the Englishman, dashing away the brushwood with the muzzle of his gun, and detecting with a quick eye the broken twigs or disturbed leaves which betrayed the course of the hunted bear. There was also something characteristic in the wearing of his dress, in the fox-skin cap thrown carelessly on one side of his superb head, exposing a mass of short brown curls around the left ear and temple, and in the bosom of his coarse frock thrown open so as to give free motion to a neck Apollo might have coveted. He was a hunter, who had occasionally visited the settlement of late, but spent whole weeks in the woods, professedly in collecting furs by his own efforts, or by purchase from the tribe of Indians encamped at the foot of the mountains.

The last was more sedate in his looks, and less buoyant in his air. There was an intellectual expression in his high, thoughtful brow, embrowned though it was by exposure. A depth of thought in his serious eye and a graceful dignity in his carriage, bespoke him as one of those who hide deep feeling under an appearance of coldness and apathy. He had been a schoolmaster in the Bay State, from whence he had been drawn by the bright eyes and merry laugh of one Martha Fellows, a maiden of seventeen, whose father had moved to the settlement at Catskill the preceding summer, and to whom, report said, he was to be married whenever a minister, authorized to perform the ceremony, should find his way to the settlement.

The three hunters bent their way in a southwestern direction from the settlement, till the forest suddenly opened into a beautiful and secluded piece of meadow-land, known to this day by its Dutch title of "the Straka," which means, our aged friends informed us, a strip of land. The Straka lay before them of an oblong form, some eight or ten acres in

4

expanse, with all its luxuriance of trees, grass and flowers, bathed in the dew and sunshine of a summer's morning. It presented a lovely contrast to the dense wilderness from which the hunters emerged, and they halted for a moment beneath the boughs of a tall hickory to enjoy its delicious freshness. The surface of the inclosure was not exactly level, but down the whole length it curved gently up from the middle, on either side, to the magnificent trees that hedged it in with a beautiful and leafy rampart. The margin was irregular; here and there a clump of trees shot down into the inclosure, and the clearing occasionally ran up into the forest in tiny glades and little grassy nooks, in which the sunlight slumbered like smiles on the face of a dreaming infant. On every side the trunks of huge trees shot up along the margin beneath their magnificent canopy of leaves, like the ivied columns of a ruin, or fell back in the misty perspective of the forest, scarcely discernible in its gloom of shadow. The heavy piles of foliage, which fell amid the boughs like a wealth of drapery flung in masses to the summer wind, was thrifty and ripe with the warm breath of August. No spirit of decay had as yet shed a gorgeous breath over its deep, rich green, but all was wet with dew, and kindled up by the sunlight to a thousand varying tints of the same color. A bright spring gushed from a swell of ground in the upper part of the inclosure, and the whole surface of the beautiful spot was covered with a vigorous growth of tall meadow-grass, which rose thicker and brighter and of a more delicate green down the middle, where the spring curved onward in a graceful rivulet, musical as the laugh of a child. As if called to life by the chime of a little brook, a host of white wild flowers unfolded their starry blossoms along the margin, and clumps of swamp lilies shed an azure hue along the grass.

Until that day, our hunters had ever found "the Straka" silent and untenanted, save by singing-birds, and wild deer which came down from the mountains to feed on its rich verdure; but now a dozen wreaths of smoke curled up from the trees at the northern extremity, and a camp of newly-erected wigwams might be seen through a vista in the wood. One or two were built even on the edge of the clearing; the grass was much trampled around them, and three or four half-naked Indian children lay rolling upon it, laughing, shouting, and flinging up their limbs in the pleasant morning air. One young Indian woman was also frolicking among them, tossing an infant in her arms, caroling and playing with it. Her laugh was musical as a bird song, and as she darted to and fro, now into the forest and then out into the sunshine, her long hair glowed like the wing of a raven, and her motion was graceful as an untamed gazelle. They could see that the child, too, was very beautiful, even from the distance at which they stood, and occasionally, as the wind swept toward them, his shout came ringing upon it like the gush of waters leaping from their fount.

"This is a little *too* bad," muttered the Englishman, fingering his gun-lock. "Can they find no spot to burrow in but 'the Straka?' St. George! but I have a mind to shoot the squaw and wring the neck of every red imp among them."

"Do it!" exclaimed Danforth, turning furiously upon him; "touch but a hair of her head, and by the Lord that made me, I will bespatter that tree with your brains!"

The Englishman dropped the stock of his musket hard to the ground, and a spot of fiery red flashed into his cheek at this savage burst of anger so uncalled for and so insolent. He gazed a moment on the frowning face of the young hunter, and then lifting his gun, turned carelessly away.

"Tut, man, have done with this," he said; "I did but jest. Come, we have lost the trail, and shall miss the game, too, if we tarry longer; come."

The Englishman shouldered his musket, as he spoke, and turned into the woods. Jones followed, but Danforth lingered behind.

"I must see what this means," he muttered, glancing after his companions, and then at the group of young Indians; "what can have brought them so near the settlement?"

He gave another quick glance toward the hunters, and then hurried across "the Straka" toward the wigwams. Jones and the Englishman had reached the little lake or pond, which was about a mile south of "the Straka," when they were again joined by Danforth. His brow was unclouded, and he seemed anxious to do away the effect of his late violence by more than ordinary cheerfulness. Harmony was restored, and they again struck into the trail of the bear, and pursued toward the mountains.

Noon found our hunters deep in the ravines which cut into the ridge of the Catskill on which the Mountain House now stands. Occupied by the wild scenery which surrounded him, Jones became separated from his companions, and long before he was aware of it, they had proceeded far beyond the reach of his voice. When he became sensible of his situation, he found himself in a deep ravine sunk into the very heart of the mountains. A small stream crept along the rocky bottom, untouched by a single sun's ray, though it was now high noon. Every thing about him was wild and fearfully sublime, but the shadows were refreshing and cool, and the stream, rippling along its rocky bed, sent up a pleasant murmur as he passed. Gradually a soft, flowing sound, like the rush of a current of air through a labyrinth of leaves and blossoms came gently to his ear. As he proceeded, it became more musical and liquid swelled upon the ear gradually and with a richer burden of sound, till he knew that it was the rush and leap of waters at no great distance. The ravine had sunk deeper and deeper, and fragments of rock lay thickly in the bed of the stream. Arthur Jones paused, and looked about him bewildered, and yet with a lofty, poetical feeling at his heart, aroused by a sense of the glorious handiwork of the Almighty encompassing him. He stood within the heart of the mountain, and it seemed to heave and tremble beneath his feet with some unknown influence as he gazed. Precipices, and rocks piled on rocks were heaped to the sky on either side. Large forest-trees stood rooted in the wide clefts, and waved their heavy boughs abroad like torn banners streaming upon the air. A strip of the blue heavens arched gently over the whole, and that was beautiful. It smiled softly, and like a promise of love over that sunless ravine. Another step, and the waterfall was before him. It was sublime, but beautiful—oh, very beautiful—that little body of water, curling and foaming downward like a wreath of snow sifted from the clouds, breaking in a shower of spray over the shelf of rocks which stayed its progress, then leaping a second foaming mass, down, down, like a deluge of flowing light, another hundred feet to the shadowy depths of the ravine. A shower of sunlight played amid the foliage far overhead, and upon the top of the curving precipice where the waters made their first leap. As the hunter became more calm, he remarked how harmoniously the beautiful and sublime were blended in the scene. The precipices were rugged and frowning, but soft, rich mosses and patches of delicate white wild-flowers clung about them. So profusely were those gentle flowers lavished upon the rocks, that it seemed as if the very spray drops were breaking into blossoms as they fell. The hunter's heart swelled with pleasure as he drank in the extreme beauty of the scene. He rested his gun against a fragment of rock, and sat down with his eyes fixed on the waterfall. As he gazed, it seemed as if the precipices were moving upward—upward to the very sky. He was pondering on this strange optical illusion, which has puzzled many a dizzy brain since, when the click of a gunlock struck sharply on his ear. He sprang to his feet. A bullet whistled by his head, cutting through the dark locks which curled in heavy masses above his temples, and as a sense of giddiness cleared from his brain, he saw a half-naked savage crouching upon the ledge of rocks which ran along the foot of the fall. The spray fell upon his bronzed shoulders and sprinkled the stock of his musket as he lifted it to discharge the other barrel. With the quickness of thought, Jones drew his musket to his eye and fired. The savage sent forth a fierce, wild yell of agony, and springing up with the bound of a wild animal, fell headlong from the shelf. Trembling with excitement, yet firm and courageous, the hunter reloaded his gun, and stood ready to sell his life as dearly as possible, for he believed that the ravine was full of concealed savages, who would fall upon him like a pack of wolves. But everything remained quiet, and when he found that he was alone, a terrible consciousness of bloodshed came upon him. His knees trembled, his cheek burned, and, with an impulse of fierce excitement, he leaped over the intervening rocks and stood by the slain savage. He was lying with his face to the earth, quite dead; Jones drew forth his knife, and lifting the long, black hair, cut it away from the crown. With the trophy in his hand, he sprang across the ravine. The fearless spirit of a madness seemed upon him, for he rushed up the steep ascent, and plunged into the forest, apparently careless what direction he took. The sound of a musket stopped his aimless career. He listened, and bent his steps more calmly toward the eminence on which the Mountain House now stands. Here he found the Englishman with the carcass of a huge bear stretched at his feet, gazing on the glorious expanse of country, spread out like a map, hundreds of fathoms beneath him. His face was flushed, and the perspiration rolled freely from his forehead. Danforth stood beside him, also bearing traces of recent conflict.

"So you have come to claim a share of the meat," said the old hunter, as Jones approached. "It is brave to leave your skulking place in the bushes, when the danger is over. Bless me, lad! what have you there?" he exclaimed, starting up and pointing to the scalp.

Jones related his encounter with the savage. The Englishman shook his head forebodingly.

"We shall have hot work for this job before the week is over," he said. "It was a foolish shot; but keep a good heart, my lad, for hang me, if I should not have done the same thing if the red devil had sent a bullet so near my head. Come, we will go and bury the fellow the best way we can."

Jones led the way to the fall, but they found only a few scattered locks of black hair, and a pool of blood half washed from the rock by the spray. The body of the savage and his rifle had disappeared—how, it was in vain to conjecture.

One of the largest log-houses in the settlement had been appropriated as a kind of tavern, or place of meeting for the settlers when they returned from their hunting excursions. Here a store of spirits was kept, under the care of John Fellows and pretty Martha Fellows, his daughter, the maiden before mentioned. As the sun went down, the men who had gone to the woods in the morning began to collect with their game. Two stags, racoons and meaner game in abundance, were lying before the door, when the three hunters came in with the slain bear. They were greeted with a boisterous shout, and the hunters crowded eagerly forward to examine the prize; but when Jones cast the Indian's scalp on the pile, they looked in each other's faces with ominous silence, while the young hunter stood pale and collected before them. It was the first time that Indian life had been taken by any of their number, and they felt that in the shedding of red blood, the barriers of their protection were broken down.

"It is a bad business," said one of the elder settlers, waving his head and breaking the general silence. "There'll be no clear hunting in the woods after this; but how did it all come about, Jones? Let us know how you came by that scalp—did the varmint fire at you, or how was it?"

The hunters gathered around Jones, who was about to account for his possession of the scalp, when the door of the house was opened, and he happened to look into the little room thus exposed. It was scantily furnished with a few benches and stools; a bed was in one corner, and Martha Fellows, his promised wife, stood by a rough, deal-table, on

7

which were two or three drinking-cups, a couple of half-empty bottles, with a pitcher of water, backed by a broken mug, filled to the fractured top with maple molasses. Nothing of the kind could have been more beautiful than pretty Martha as she bent forward, listening with rapt attention to the animated whisper of William Danforth, who stood by her, divested of his coarse frock, his cap lying on the table before him, and his athletic figure displayed to the best advantage by the roundabout buttoned closely over his bosom. A red silk handkerchief, tied like a scarf round his waist, gave a picturesque gracefulness to his costume, altogether in harmony with his fine proportions, and with the bold cast of his head, which certainly was a model of muscular beauty.

A flash of anger shot athwart Arthur Jones' forehead, and a strange jealous feeling came to his heart. He began a confused account of his adventure, but the Englishman interrupted him, and took it upon himself to gratify the clamorous curiosity of the hunters, leaving Jones at liberty to scrutinize each look and motion of his lady-love. He watched with a jealous feeling the blush as it deepened and glowed on her embrowned cheek; he saw the sparkling pleasure of her hazel eyes, and the pretty dimples gathering about her red lips, like spots of sunlight flickering through the leaves of a red rose, and his heart sickened with distrust. But when the handsome hunter laid his hands on hers and bent his head, till the short curls on his temples almost mingled with her glossy ringlets, the lover could bear the sight no more. Breaking from the little band of hunters, he stalked majestically into the house, and approaching the object of his uneasiness, exclaimed, "Martha Fellows," in a voice which caused the pretty culprit to snatch her hand from under the hunter's, and to overturn two empty tin cups in her fright.

"Sir," said Martha, recovering herself, and casting a mischievous glance at Danforth, which was reciprocated with interest.

Mr. Arthur Jones felt that he was making himself ridiculous, and suppressing his wrath, he finished his magnificent commencement; "Will you give me a drink of water?" At which Martha pointed with her little embrowned hand to the pitcher, saying:

"There it is;" then, turning her back to her lover, she cast another arch glance at Danforth, and taking his cap from the table, began to blow upon the yellow fur, and put it to her cheek, as if it had been a pet kitten she was caressing, and all for the laudable purpose of tormenting the man who loved her, and whom she loved better than any thing in existence. Jones turned on her a bitter contemptuous look, and raising the pitcher to his lips, left the room. In a few minutes the other hunters entered, and Jason Fellows, father to Martha, announced it as decided by the hunters, who had been holding a kind of council without, that Arthur Jones and William Danforth, as the two youngest members of the community, should be dispatched to the nearest settlement to request aid to protect them from the Indians, whose immediate attack they had good reason to fear.

Martha, on hearing the names of the emissaries mentioned, dropped the cup she had been filling.

"Oh, not him—not them, I mean—they will be overtaken and tomahawked by the way!" she exclaimed, turning to her father with a look of affright.

"Let Mr. Danforth remain," said Jones, advancing to the table; "I will undertake the mission alone."

Tears came into Martha's eyes, and she turned them reproachfully to her lover; but, full of his heroic resolution to be tomahawked and comfortably scalped on his own responsibility, he turned majestically, without deigning to meet the tearful glance which was well calculated to mitigate his jealous wrath.

Danforth, on being applied to, requested permission to defer his answer till the morning, and the hunters left the house to divide the game, which had been forgotten in the general excitement.

8

Danforth, who had lingered to the last, took up his cap, and whispering good-night to Martha, left the house. The poor girl scarcely heeded his departure. Her eyes filled with tears, and seating herself on a settee which ran along one end of the room, she folded her arms on a board which served as a back, and burying her face upon them, wept violently.

As she remained in this position, she heard a familiar step on the floor. Her heart beat quick, fluttered a moment, and then settled to its regular pulsations again, for her lover had seated himself beside her. Martha wiped the tears from her eyes and remained quiet, for she knew that he had returned, and with that knowledge, the spirit of coquetry had revived; and when Jones, softened by her apparent sorrow—for he had seen her parting with Danforth—put his hand softly under her forehead and raised her face, the creature was laughing—laughing at his folly, as he thought.

"Martha, you are doing wrong—wrong to yourself and to me," said the disappointed lover, rising indignantly and taking his hat, with which he advanced to the door.

"Don't go," said Martha, turning her head till one cheek only rested on her arm, and casting a glance, half-repentant, half-comic, on her retreating lover; "don't go off so; if you do, you'll be very sorry for it."

Jones hesitated—she became very serious—the tears sprang to her eyes, and she looked exceedingly penitent. He returned to her side. Had he appealed to her feelings then—had he spoken of the pain she had given him in her encouragement of another, she would have acknowledged the fault with all proper humility; but he did no such thing—he was a common-sense man, and he resolved to end his first love-quarrel in a common-sense manner, as if common-sense ever had any thing to do with lovers' quarrels. "I will reason with her," he thought. "He will say I have made him very wretched, and I will tell him I am very sorry," *she* thought.

"Martha," he said, very deliberately, "why do I find you on terms of such familiarity with this Manhattan fellow?"

Martha was disappointed. He spoke quite too calmly, and there was a sarcastic emphasis in the word "fellow," that roused her pride. The lips, which had just begun to quiver with repentance, worked themselves into a pouting fullness, till they resembled the rose-bud just as it bursts into leaves. Her rounded shoulder was turned pettishly toward her lover, with the air of a spoiled child, and she replied that "he was always finding fault."

Jones took her hand, and was proceeding in his sensible manner to convince her that she was wrong, and acted wildly, foolishly, and with a careless disregard to her own happiness.

As might be expected, the beautiful rustic snatched her hand away, turned her shoulder more decidedly on her lover, and bursting into tears, declared that she would thank him if he would stop scolding, and that she did not care if she never set eyes on him again.

He would have remonstrated; "Do listen to common sense," he said, extending his hand to take hers.

"I hate common-sense!" she exclaimed, dashing away his hand; "I won't hear any more of your lecturing,—leave the house, and never speak to me again as long as you live."

Mr. Arthur Jones took up his hat, placed it deliberately on his head, and walked out of the house. With a heavy heart Martha watched his slender form as it disappeared in the darkness, and then stole away to her bed in the garret.

"He will call in the morning before he starts; he won't have the heart to go away without saying one word,—I am sure he won't," she repeated to herself over and over again, as she lay sobbing and weeping penitent tears on her pillow that night.

9

When William left the log tavern, he struck into the woods, and took his course toward the Pond. There was a moon, but the sky was clouded, and the little light which struggled to the earth, was too faint to penetrate the thick foliage of the wilderness. Danforth must have been familiar with the track, for he found his way without difficulty through the wilderness, and never stopped till he came out on the northern brink of the Pond. He looked anxiously over the face of the little lake. The fitful moon had broken from a cloud, and was touching the tiny waves with beauty, while the broken, rocky shore encompassed it with shadow, like a frame-work of ebony. No speck was on its bosom; no sound was abroad, but the evening breeze as it rippled on the waters, and made a sweet whispering melody in the tree-tops.

Suddenly a light, as from a pine torch, was seen on a point of land jutting out from the opposite shore. Another and another flashed out, each bearing to a particular direction, and then a myriad of flames rose high and bright, illuminating the whole point, and shooting its fiery reflection, like a meteor, almost across the bosom of the waters.

"Yes, they are preparing for work," muttered Danforth, as he saw a crowd of painted warriors arrange themselves around the camp-fire, each with his firelock in his hand. There was a general movement. Dark faces flitted in quick succession between him and the blaze as the warriors performed the heavy march, or war-dance, which usually preceded the going out of a hostile party.

Danforth left the shore, and striking out in an oblique direction, arrived, after half an hour of quick walking, at the Indian encampment. He threaded his way through the cluster of bark wigwams, till he came to one standing on the verge of the inclosure. It was of logs, and erected with a regard to comfort which the others wanted. The young hunter drew aside the mat which hung over the entrance, and looked in. A young Indian girl was sitting on a pile of furs at the opposite extremity. She wore no paint—her cheek was round and smooth, and large gazelle-like eyes gave a soft brilliancy to her countenance, beautiful beyond expression. Her dress was a robe of dark chintz, open at the throat, and confined at the waist by a narrow belt of wampum, which, with the bead bracelets on her naked arms, and the embroidered moccasins laced over her feet, was the only Indian ornament about her. Even her hair, which all of her tribe wore laden with ornaments, and hanging down the back, was braided and wreathed in raven bands over her smooth forehead. An infant, almost naked, was lying in her lap, throwing its unfettered limbs about, and lifting his little hands to his mother's mouth, as she rocked back and forth on her seat of skins, chanting, in a sweet, mellow voice, the burden of an Indian lullaby. As the form of the hunter darkened the entrance, the Indian girl started up with a look of affectionate joy, and lying her child on the pile of skins, advanced to meet him.

"Why did the white man leave his woman so many nights?" she said, in her broken English, hanging fondly about him; "the boy and his mother have listened long for the sound of his moccasins."

Danforth passed his arm around the waist of his Indian wife, and drawing her to him bent his cheek to hers, as if that slight caress was sufficient answer to her gentle greeting, and so it was; her untutored heart, rich in its natural affections, had no aim, no object, but what centered in the love she bore her white husband. The feelings which in civilized life are scattered over a thousand objects, were, in her bosom, centered in one single being; he supplied the place of all the high aspirations—of all the passions and sentiments which are fostered into strength by society, and as her husband bowed his head to hers, the blood darkened her cheek, and her large liquid eyes were flooded with delight.

"And what has Malaeska been doing since the boy's father went to the wood?" inquired Danforth, as she drew him to the couch where the child was lying half buried in the rich fur.

"Malaeska has been alone in the wigwam, watching the shadow of the big pine. When her heart grew sick, she looked in the boy's eyes and was glad," replied the Indian mother, laying the infant in his father's arms.

Danforth kissed the child, whose eyes certainly bore a striking resemblance to his own; and parting the straight, black hair from a forehead which scarcely bore a tinge of its mother's blood, muttered, "It's a pity the little fellow is not quite white."

The Indian mother took the child, and with a look of proud anguish, laid her finger on its cheek, which was rosy with English blood.

"Malaeska's father is a great chief—the boy will be a chief in her father's tribe; but Malaeska never thinks of that when she sees the white man's blood come into the boy's face." She turned mournfully to her seat again.

"He will make a brave chief," said Danforth, anxious to soften the effects of his inadvertent speech; "but tell me, Malaeska, why have the warriors kindled the council fire? I saw it blaze by the pond as I came by."

Malaeska could only inform that the body of a dead Indian had been brought to the encampment about dusk, and that it was supposed he had been shot by some of the whites from the settlement. She said that the chief had immediately called a council to deliberate on the best means of revenging their brother's death.

Danforth had feared this movement in the savages, and it was to mitigate their wrath that he sought the encampment at so late an hour. He had married the daughter of their chief, and, consequently, was a man of considerable importance in the tribe. But he felt that his utmost exertion might fail to draw them from their meditated vengeance, now that one of their number had been slain by the whites. Feeling the necessity of his immediate presence at the council, he left the wigwam and proceeded at a brisk walk to the brink of the Pond. He came out of the thick forest which fringed it a little above the point on which the Indians were collected. Their dance was over, and from the few guttural tones which reached him, Danforth knew that they were planning the death of some particular individuals, which was probably to precede their attack on the settlement. The council fire still streamed high in the air, reddening the waters and lighting up the trees and foreground with a beautiful effect, while the rocky point seemed of emerald pebbles, so brilliant was the reflection cast over it, and so distinctly did it display the painted forms of the savages as they sat in a circle round the blaze, each with his weapon lying idly by his side. The light lay full on the glittering wampum and feathery crest of one who was addressing them with more energy than is common to the Indian warrior.

Danforth was too far off to collect a distinct hearing of the discourse, but with a feeling of perfect security, he left the deep shadow in which he stood, and approached the council fire. As the light fell upon him, the Indians leaped to their feet, and a savage yell rent the air, as if a company of fiends had been disturbed in their orgies. Again and again was the fierce cry reiterated, till the woods resounded with the wild echo rudely summoned from the caves. As the young hunter stood lost in astonishment at the strange commotion, he was seized by the savages, and dragged before their chief, while the group around furiously demanded vengeance, quick and terrible, for the death of their slain brother. The truth flashed across the hunter's mind. It was death they had been planning. It was he they supposed to be the slayer of the Indian. He remonstrated and declared himself guiltless of the red man's death. It was in vain. He had been seen on the mountain by one of the tribe, not five minutes before the dead body of the Indian was found. Almost in despair the hunter turned to the chief.

"Am I not your son—the father of a young chief—one of your own tribe?" he said, with appealing energy.

The saturnine face of the chief never changed, as he answered in his own language: "The red man has taken a rattlesnake to warm in his wigwam—the warrior shall crush his head!" and with a fierce grin, he pointed to the pile of resinous wood which the savages were heaping on the council fire.

Danforth looked around on the group preparing for his destruction. Every dusky face was lighted up with a demoniac thirst for blood, the hot flames quivering into the air, their gorgeous tints amalgamating and shooting upward like a spire of living rainbows, while a thousand fiery tongues, hissing and darting onward like vipers eager for their prey, licked the fresh pine-knots heaped for his death-pyre. It was a fearful sight, and the heart of the brave hunter quailed within him as he looked. With another wild whoop, the Indians seized their victim, and were about to strip him for the sacrifice. In their blind fury, they tore him from the grasp of those who held him, and were too intent on divesting him of his clothes to remark that his limbs were free. But he was not so forgetful. Collecting his strength for a last effort, he struck the nearest savage a blow in the chest, which sent him reeling among his followers, then taking advantage of the confusion, he tore off his cap, and springing forward with the bound of an uncaged tiger, plunged into the lake. A shout rent the air, and a score of dark heads broke the water in pursuit.

Fortunately a cloud was over the moon and the fugitive remained under the water till he reached the shadow thrown by the thickly-wooded bank, when, rising for a moment, he supported himself and hurled his cap out toward the center of the pond. The ruse succeeded, for the moon came out just at the instant, and with renewed shouts the savages turned in pursuit of the empty cap. Before they learned their mistake, Danforth had made considerable headway under the friendly bank, and took the woods just as the shoal of Indians' heads entered the shadow in eager chase.

The fugitive stood for a moment on the brink of the forest, irresolute, for he knew not which course to take.

"I have it; they will never think of looking for me there," he exclaimed, dashing through the undergrowth, and taking the direction toward "the Straka." The whoop of the pursuers smote his ear as they made the land. On, on he bounded with the swiftness of a hunted stag, through swamp and brushwood, and over rocks. He darted till he came in sight of his own wigwam. The sound of pursuit had died away, and he began to hope that the savages had taken the track which led to the settlement.

Breathless with exertions he entered the hut. The boy was asleep, but his mother was listening for the return of her husband.

"Malaeska," he said, catching her to his panting heart: "Malaeska, we must part; your tribe seek my life; warriors are on my track now—now! Do you hear their shouts?" he added.

A wild whoop came up from the woods below, and forcing back the arms she had flung about him, he seized a war-club and stood ready for the attack.

Malaeska sprang to the door, and looked out with the air of a frightened doe. Darting back to the pile of furs, she laid the sleeping child on the bare earth, and motioning her husband to lie down, heaped the skins over his prostrate form; then taking the child in her arms, she stretched herself on the pile, and drawing a bear-skin over her, pretended to be asleep. She had scarcely composed herself, when three savages entered the wigwam. One bore a blazing pine-knot, with which he proceeded to search for the fugitive. While the others were busy among the scanty furniture, he approached the trembling wife, and after feeling about among the furs without effect, lifted the bear-skins which covered her; but her sweet face in apparent slumber, and the beautiful infant lying across her bosom, were all that rewarded his search. As if her beauty had power to tame the savage, he carefully replaced the covering over her person, and speaking to his companions, left the hut without attempting to disturb her further.

Malaeska remained in her feigned slumber till she heard the Indians take to the woods again. Then she arose and lifted the skins from off her husband, who was nearly suffocated under them. When he had regained his feet, she placed the war-club in his hand, and taking up the babe, led the way to the entrance of the hut. Danforth saw by the act, that she intended to desert her tribe and accompany him in his flight. He had never thought of introducing her as his wife among the whites, and now that circumstances made it necessary for him to part with her forever, or to take her among his people for a shelter, a pang, such as he had never felt, came to his heart. His affections struggled powerfully with his pride. The picture of his disgrace—of the scorn with which his parents and sisters would receive the Indian wife and half Indian child, presented itself before him, and he had not the moral courage to risk the degradation which her companionship would bring upon him. These conflicting thoughts flashed through his mind in an instant, and when his wife stopped at the door, and, looking anxiously in his face, beckoned him to follow, he said, sharply, for his conscience was ill at ease:

"Malaeska, I go alone; you and the boy must remain with your people."

His words had a withering effect on the poor Indian. Her form drooped, and she raised her eyes with a look so mingled with humiliation and reproach, that the hunter's heart thrilled painfully in his bosom. Slowly, and as if her soul and strength were paralyzed, she crept to her husband's feet, and sinking to her knees, held up the babe.

"Malaeska's breast will die, and the boy will have no one to feed him," she said.

That beautiful child—that young mother kneeling in her humiliation—those large dark eyes, dim with the intensity of her solicitude, and that voice so full of tender entreaty—the husband's heart could not withstand them. His bosom heaved, tears gathered in his eyes, and raising the Indian and her child to his bosom, he kissed them both again and again.

"Malaeska," he said, folding her close to his heart, "Malaeska, I must go now; but when seven suns have passed, I will come again; or, if the tribe still seek my life, take the child and come to the settlement. I shall be there."

The Indian woman bowed her head in humble submission.

"The white man is good. Malaeska will come," she said.

One more embrace, and the poor Indian wife was alone with her child.

Poor Martha Fellows arose early, and waited with nervous impatience for the appearance of her lover; but the morning passed, the hour of noon drew near, and he came not. The heart of the maiden grew heavy, and when her father came in to dine, her eyes were red with weeping, and a cloud of mingled sorrow and petulance darkened her handsome face. She longed to question her father about Jones, but he had twice replenished his brown earthern bowl with pudding and milk, before she could gather courage to speak.

"Have you seen Arthur Jones this morning?" she at length questioned in a low, timid voice.

The answer she received, was quite sufficient punishment for all her coquettish folly of the previous night. Jones had left the settlement—left it in anger with her, without a word of explanation—without even saying farewell. It really was hard. The little coquette had the heart-ache terribly, till he frightened it away by telling her of the adventure which Danforth had met with among the Indians, and of his departure with Arthur Jones in search of aid from the nearest settlement. The old man gloomily added, that the savages would doubtless burn the houses over their heads, and massacre every living being within them, long before the two brave fellows would return with men. Such indeed, were the terrible fears of almost every one in the little neighborhood. Their apprehensions however, were premature. Part of the Indian tribe had gone out on a hunting-party among the hills, and were ignorant of the fatal shot with which Jones had aroused the animosity of their brethren; while those who remained, were dispersed in a fruitless pursuit after Danforth.

On the afternoon of the fifth day after the departure of their emissaries, the whites began to see unequivocal symptoms of an attack; and now their fears did not deceive them. The hunting-party had returned to their encampment, and the detached parties were gathering around "the Straka." About dark, an Indian appeared in the skirts of the clearing, as if to spy out the position of the whites. Soon after, a shot was fired at the Englishman, before mentioned as he returned from his work, which passed through the crown of his hat. That hostilities were commencing, was now beyond a doubt, and the males of the settlement met in solemn conclave, to devise measures for the defence of their wives and children. Their slender preparations were soon made; all were gathered around one of the largest houses in gloomy apprehension; the women and children within, and the man standing in front, sternly resolving to die in the defence of their loved ones. Suddenly there came up a sound from the wood, the trampling of many feet, and the crackling of brushwood, as if some large body of men were forcing a way through the tangled forest. The women bowed their pallid faces, and gathering their children in their arms, waited appalled for the attack. The men stood ready, each grasping his weapon, their faces pallid, and their eyes kindled with stern courage, as they heard the stifled groans of the loved objects cowering behind them for protection. The sound became nearer and more distinct; dark forms were seen dimly moving among the trees, and then a file of men came out into the clearing. They were whites, led on by William Danforth and Arthur Jones. The settlers uttered a boisterous shout, threw down their arms, and ran in a body to meet the new-comers. The woman sprang to their feet, some weeping, others laughing in hysterical joy, and all embracing their children with frantic energy.

Never were there more welcome guests than the score of weary men who refreshed themselves in the various houses of the settlement that night. Sentinels were placed, and each settler returned to his dwelling, accompanied by three or four guests; every heart beat high, save one—Martha Fellows; she, poor girl, was sad among the general rejoicing; her lover had not spoken to her though she lingered near his side in the crowd, and had once almost touched him. Instead of going directly to her father's house, as had been his custom, he accepted the Englishman's invitation, and departed to sleep in his dwelling.

Now this same Englishman had a niece residing with him, who was considered by some to be more beautiful than Martha herself. The humble maiden thought of Jones, and of the bright blue eyes of the English girl, till her heart burned with the same jealous feelings she had so ridiculed in her lover.

"I will see him! I will see them both!" she exclaimed, starting up from the settle where she had remained, full of jealous anxiety, since the dispersing of the crowd; and unheeded by her father, who was relating his hunting exploits to the five strangers quartered on him, she dashed away her tears, threw a shawl over her head, and taking a cup, as an excuse for borrowing something, left the house.

The Englishman's dwelling stood on the outward verge of the clearing, just within the shadow of the forest. Martha had almost reached the entrance, when a dark form rushed

14

from its covert in the brushwood, and rudely seizing her, darted back into the wilderness. The terrified girl uttered a fearful shriek; for the fierce eyes gazing down upon her, were those of a savage. She could not repeat the cry, for the wretch crushed her form to his naked chest with a grasp of iron, and winding his hand in her hair, was about to dash her to the ground. That moment a bullet whistled by her cheek. The Indian tightened his hold with spasmodic violence, staggered back, and fell to the ground, still girding her in his death-grasp; a moment he writhed in mortal agony—warm blood gushed over his victim—the heart under her struggled fiercely in its last throes; then the lifeless arms relaxed, and she lay fainting on a corpse.

CHAPTER II.

He lay upon the trampled ground, She knelt beside him there, While a crimson stream gush'd slowly 'Neath the parting of his hair. His head was on her bosom thrown— She sobb'd his Christian name— He smiled, for still he knew her, And strove to do the same.—Frank Lee Benedict.

"Oh, Arthur! dear Arthur, I am glad it was you that saved me," whispered Martha, about an hour after her rescue, as she lay on the settle in her father's house, with Arthur Jones bending anxiously over her.

Jones dropped the hand he had been holding and turned away with troubled features.

Martha looked at him, and her eyes were brimming with tears. "Jones," she said humbly and very affectionately, "Jones, I did wrong the other night, and I am sorry for it; will you forgive me?"

"I will—but never again—never, as I live," he replied, with a stern determination in his manner, accompanied by a look that humbled her to the heart. In after years, when Martha was Arthur Jones' wife, and when the stirrings of vanity would have led her to trifle with his feelings, she remembered that look, and dared not brave it a second time.

At sunrise, the next morning, an armed force went into the forest, composed of all who could be spared from the settlement, amounting to about thirty fighting-men. The Indians, encamped about "the Straka," more than doubled that number, yet the handful of brave whites resolved to offer them a decisive combat.

The little band was approaching the northeastern extremity of the Pond, when they halted for a moment to rest. The spot on which they stood was level, and thinly timbered. Some were sitting on the grass, and others leaning on their guns, consulting on their future movements, when a fiendish yell arose like the howl of a thousand wild beasts, and, as if the very earth had yawned to emit them, a band of warriors sprang up in appalling numbers, on the front and rear, and approaching them, three abreast, fired into the group with terrible slaughter.

The whites returned their fire, and the sounds of murderous strife were indeed horrible. Sternly arose the white man's shout amid the blazing of guns and the whizzing of tomahawks, as they flashed through the air on their message of blood. Above all burst out the war-whoop of the savages, sometimes rising hoarse, and like the growling of a thousand bears; then, as the barking of as many wolves, and again, sharpening to the shrill, unearthly cry of a tribe of wildcats. Oh, it was fearful, that scene of slaughter. Heart to heart, and muzzle to muzzle, the white and red man battled in horrid strife. The trees above them drooped under a cloud of smoke, and their trunks were scarred with

15

gashes, cut by the tomahawks which had missed their more deadly aim. The ground was burdened with the dead, and yet the strife raged fiercer and fiercer till the going down of the sun.

In the midst of the fight was William Danforth. Many a dusky form bit the dust, and many a savage howl followed the discharge of his trusty gun. But at length it became foul with continued use, and he went to the brink of the Pond to wash it. He was stooping to the water, when the dark form of an Indian chief cast its shadow a few feet from him. He, too, had come down to clean his gun. The moment he had accomplished his purpose, he turned to the white man, who had been to him as a son, and drawing his muscular form up to its utmost height, uttered a defiance in the Indian tongue. Instantly the weapons of both were loaded and discharged. The tall form of the chief wavered unsteadily for a moment, and fell forward, half its length, into the Pond. He strove to rise. His hands dashed wildly on the crimson water, the blows grew fainter, and the chief was dead.

The setting sun fell brilliantly over the glittering raiment of the prostrate chief—his long, black hair streamed out upon the water, and the tiny waves rippled playfully among the gorgeous feathers which had been his savage crown. A little back, on the green bank, lay Danforth, wounded unto death. He strove to creep to the battle-field, but the blood gushed afresh from his wounds, and he fell back upon the earth faint and in despair.

The savages retreated; the sounds of strife became more distant, and the poor youth was left alone with the body of the slain warrior. He made one more desperate effort, and secured the gun which had belonged to the chief; though faint with loss of blood, he loaded that as well as his own, and placing them beside him, resolved to defend the remnant of life, yet quivering at his heart, to the last moment. The sun went slowly down; the darkness fell like a vail over the like, and there he lay, wounded and alone, in the solitude of the wilderness. Solemn and regretful were the thoughts of the forsaken man as that night of agony went by. Now his heart lingered with strange and terrible dread around the shadowy portals of eternity which were opening before him; again it turned with a strong feeling of self-condemnation to his Indian wife and the infant pledge of the great love, which had made him almost forsake kindred and people for their sakes.

The moon arose, and the dense shadow of a hemlock, beneath which he had fallen, lay within a few feet of him like the wing of a great bird, swayed slowly forward with an imperceptible and yet certain progress. The eyes of the dying man were fixed on the margin of the shadow with a keen, intense gaze. There was something terrible in its stealthy creeping and silent advance, and he strove to elude it as if it had been a living thing; but with every motion the blood gushed afresh from his heart, and he fell back upon the sod, his white teeth clenched with pain, and his hands clutched deep into the damp moss. Still his keen eyes glittered in the moonlight with the fevered workings of pain and imagination. The shadow on which they turned was to him no shadow, but now a nest of serpents, creeping with their insidious coils toward him; and again, a pall—a black funereal pall, dragged forward by invisible spirits, and about to shut him out from the light forever. Slowly and surely it crept across his damp forehead and over his glowing eyes. His teeth unclenched, his hands relaxed, and a gentle smile broke over his pale lips, when he felt with what a cool and spirit-like touch it visited him. Just then a human shadow mingled with that of the tree, and the wail of a child broke on the still night air. The dying hunter struggled and strove to cry out,—"Malaeska—Ma—Ma—Mala—"

The poor Indian girl heard the voice, and with a cry, half of frenzied joy and half of fear, sprang to his side. She flung her child on the grass and lifted her dying husband to her heart, and kissed his damp forehead in a wild, eager agony of sorrow.

"Malaeska," said the young man, striving to wind his arms about her, "my poor girl, what will become of you? O God! who will take care of my boy?"

16

The Indian girl pushed back the damp hair from his forehead, and looked wildly down into his face. A shiver ran through her frame when she saw the cold, gray shadows of death gathering there; then her black eyes kindled, her beautiful lip curved to an expression more lofty than a smile, her small hand pointed to the West, and the wild religion of her race gushed up from her heart, a stream of living poetry.

"The hunting-ground of the Indian is yonder, among the purple clouds of the evening. The stars are very thick there, and the red light is heaped together like mountains in the heart of a forest. The sugar-maple gives its waters all the year round, and the breath of the deer is sweet, for it feeds on the golden spire-bush and the ripe berries. A lake of bright waters is there. The Indian's canoe flies over it like a bird high up in the morning. The West has rolled back its clouds, and a great chief has passed through. He will hold back the clouds that his white son may go up to the face of the Great Spirit. Malaeska and her boy will follow. The blood of the red man is high in her heart, and the way is open. The lake is deep, and the arrow sharp; death will come when Malaeska calls him. Love will make her voice sweet in the land of the Great Spirit; the white man will hear it, and call her to his bosom again!"

A faint, sad smile flitted over the dying hunter's face, and her voice was choked with pain which was not death. "My poor girl," he said, feebly drawing her kindling face to his lips, "there is no great hunting-ground as you dream. The whites have another faith, and—O God! I have taken away her trust, and have none to give in return!"

The Indian's face drooped forward, the light of her wild, poetic faith had departed with the hunter's last words, and a feeling of cold desolation settled on her heart. He was dying on her bosom, and she knew not where he was going, nor that their parting might not be eternal.

The dying man's lips moved as if in prayer. "Forgive me, O Father of mercies! forgive me that I have left this poor girl in her heathen ignorance," he murmured, faintly, and his lips continued to move though there was no perceptible sound. After a few moments of exhaustion, he fixed his eyes on the Indian girl's face with a look of solemn and touching earnestness.

"Malaeska," he said, "talk not of putting yourself and the boy to death. That would be a sin, and God would punish it. To meet me in another world, Malaeska, you must learn to love the white man's God, and wait patiently till he shall send you to me. Go not back to your tribe when I am dead. Down at the mouth of the great river are many whites; among them are my father and mother. Find your way to them, tell them how their son died, and beseech them to cherish you and the boy for his sake. Tell them how much he loved you, my poor girl. Tell them—I can not talk more. There is a girl at the settlement, one Martha Fellows; go to her. She knows of you, and has papers—a letter to my father. I did not expect this, but had prepared for it. Go to her—you will do this—promise, while I can understand."

Malaeska had not wept till now, but her voice was choked, and tears fell like rain over the dying man's face as she made the promise.

He tried to thank her, but the effort died away in a faint smile and a tremulous motion of the white lips—"Kiss me, Malaeska."

The request was faint as a breath of air, but Malaeska heard it. She flung herself on his bosom with a passionate burst of grief, and her lips clung to his as if they would have drawn him back from the very grave. She felt the cold lips moving beneath the despairing pressure of hers, and lifted her head.

"The boy, Malaeska; let me look on my son."

17

The child had crept to his mother's side, and crouching on his hands and knees, sat with his large black eyes filled with a strange awe, gazing on the white face of his father. Malaeska drew him closer, and with instinctive feelings he wound his arms round the neck, and nestled his face close to the ashy cheek of the dying man. There was a faint motion of the hands as if the father would have embraced his child, and then all was still. After a time, the child felt the cheek beneath his waxing hard and cold. He lifted his head and pored with breathless wonder over the face of his father's corpse. He looked up at his mother. She, too, was bending intently over the face of the dead, and her eyes were full of a wild, melancholy light. The child was bewildered. He passed his tiny hand once more over the cold face, and then crept away, buried his head in the folds of his mother's dress, and began to cry.

Morning dawned upon the little lake, quietly and still, as if nothing but the dews of heaven and the flowers of earth had ever tasted its freshness; yet all under the trees, the tender grass and the white blossoms, were crushed to the ground, stained and trampled in human blood. The delicious light broke, like a smile from heaven, over the still bosom of the waters, and flickered cheeringly through the dewy branches of the hemlock which shadowed the prostrate hunter. Bright dew-drops lay thickly on his dress, and gleamed, like a shower of seed pearls, in his rich, brown hair. The green moss on either side was soaked with a crimson stain, and the pale, leaden hue of dissolution had settled on his features. He was not alone; for on the same mossy couch lay the body of the slaughtered chief; the limbs were composed, as if on a bier—the hair wiped smooth, and the crescent of feathers, broken and wet, were arranged with care around his bronzed temples. A little way off, on a hillock, purple with flowers, lay a beautiful child, beckoning to the birds as they fluttered by—plucking up the flowers, and uttering his tiny shout of gladness, as if death and sorrow were not all around him. There, by the side of the dead hunter, sat Malaeska, the widow, her hands dropping nervously by her side, her long hair sweeping the moss, and her face bowed on her bosom, stupefied with the overwhelming poignancy of her grief. Thus she remained, motionless and lost in sorrow, till the day was at its noon. Her child, hungry and tired with play, had cried itself to sleep among the flowers; but the mother knew it not—her heart and all her faculties seemed closed as with a portal of ice.

That night when the moon was up, the Indian widow dug a grave, with her own hands, on the green margin of the lake. She laid her husband and her father side by side, and piled sods upon them. Then she lifted the wretched and hungry babe from the earth, and, with a heavy heart, bent her way to "the Straka."

CHAPTER III.

The sunset fell to the deep, deep stream, Ruddy as gold could be, While russet brown and a crimson gleam Slept in each forest-tree; But the heart of the Indian wife was sad As she urged her light canoe, While her boy's young laugh rose high and glad When the wild birds o'er them flew.

Martha Fellows and her lover were alone in her father's cabin on the night after the Indian engagement. They were both paler than usual, and too anxious about the safety of their little village for any thing like happiness, or tranquil conversation. The old man had been stationed as sentinel on the verge of the clearing; and as the two sat together in silence, with hands interlocked, and gazing wistfully in each other's face, a rifle-shot cut sharply from the old man's station. They both started to their feet, and Martha clung shrieking to her lover. Jones forced her back to the settle—and, snatching his rifle, sprang to the door. There was a sound of approaching footsteps, and with it was mingled the voice of old Fellows, and the sweeter and more imperfect tones of a female, with the sobbing breath of a child. As Jones stood wondering at the strange sound, a remarkable group darkened the light which streamed from the cabin-door. It was Fellows partly supporting and partly dragging forward a pale and terrified Indian girl. The light glittered upon her picturesque raiment, and revealed the dark, bright eyes of a child which was fastened to her back, and which clung to her neck silent with terror and exhaustion.

"Come along, you young porcupine! You skulking copper-colored little squaw, you! We shan't kill you, nor the little pappoose, neither; so you needn't shake so. Come along! There's Martha Fellows, if you can find enough of your darnationed queer English to tell her what you want."

As he spoke, the rough, but kind-hearted old man entered the hut, pushing the wretched Malaeska and her child before him.

"Martha! why what in the name of nature makes you look so white about the mouth? You needn't be afraid of this little varmint, no how. She's as harmless as a garter-snake. Come, see if you can find out what she wants of you. She can talk the drollest you ever heard. But I've scared away her senses, and she only stares at me like a shot deer."

When the Indian heard the name of the astonished girl, into whose presence she had been dragged she withdrew from the old man's grasp and stole timidly toward the settle.

"The white man left papers with the maiden—Malaeska only wants the papers," she pleaded, placing her small palms beseechingly together.

Martha turned still more pale, and started to her feet. "It is true then," she said, almost wildly. "Poor Danforth is dead, and these forlorn creatures his widow and child, have come to me at last. Oh! Jones, he was telling me of this the night you got so angry. I could not tell you why we were talking so much together; but I knew all the time that he had an Indian wife—it seemed as if he had a forewarning of his death, and must tell some one. The last time I saw him, he gave me a letter, sealed with black, and bade me seek his wife, and persuade her to carry it to his father, if he was killed in the fight. It is that letter she has come after; but how will she find her way to Manhattan?"

"Malaeska knows which way the waters run: She can find a path down the big river. Give her the papers that she may go!" pleaded the sad voice of the Indian.

"Tell us first," said Jones, addressing her kindly, "have the Indians left our neighborhood? Is there no danger of an attack?"

"The white man need not fear. When the great chief died, the smoke of his wigwam went out; and his people have gone beyond the mountains. Malaeska is alone."

There was wretchedness and touching pathos in the poor girl's speech, that affected the little group even to tears.

"No you ain't, by gracious!" exclaimed Fellows, dashing his hand across his eyes. "You shall stay and live with me, and help Matt, you shall—and that's the end on't. I'll make a farmer of the little pappoose. I'll bet a beaver-skin that he'll larn to gee and haw the oxen and hold plow afore half the Dutch boys that are springing up here as thick as clover-tops in a third year's clearing."

Malaeska did not perfectly understand the kind settler's proposition; the tone and manner were kindly, and she knew that he wished to help her.

"When the boy's father was dying, he told Malaeska to go to his people, and they would tell her how to find the white man's God. Give her the papers, and she will go. Her heart will be full when she thinks of the kind words and the soft looks which the white chief and the bright haired maiden have given her."

"She goes to fulfill a promise to the dead—we ought not to prevent her," said Jones.

Malaeska turned her eyes eagerly and gratefully upon him as he spoke, and Martha went to her bed and drew the letter, which had been intrusted to her care, from beneath the pillow. The Indian took it between her trembling hands, and pressing it with a gesture almost of idolatry to her lips, thrust it into her bosom.

"The white maiden is good! Farewell!" she turned toward the door as she spoke.

"Stay! It will take many days to reach Manhattan—take something to eat, or you will starve on the way," said Martha, compassionately.

"Malaeska has her bow and arrow, and she can use them; but she thanks the white maiden. A piece of bread for the boy—he has cried to his mother many times for food; but her bosom was full of tears, and she had none to give him."

Martha ran to the cupboard and brought forth a large fragment of bread and a cup milk. When the child saw the food, he uttered a soft, hungry murmur, and his little fingers began to work eagerly on his mother's neck. Martha held the cup to his lips, and smiled through her tears to see how hungrily he swallowed, and with what a satisfied and pleased look his large, black eyes were turned up to hers as he drank. When the cup was withdrawn, the boy breathed a deep sigh of satisfaction, and let his head fall sleepily on his mother's shoulder; her large eyes seemed full of moonlight, and a gleam of pleasure shot athwart her sad features; she unbound a bracelet of wampum from her arm and placed it in Martha's hand. The next instant she was lost in the darkness without. The kind settler rushed out, and hallooed for her to come back; but her step was like that of a fawn, and while he was wandering fruitlessly around the settlement, she reached the margin of the creek; and, unmooring a canoe, which lay concealed in the sedge, placed herself in it, and shot round the point to the broad bosom of the Hudson.

Night and morning, for many successive days, that frail canoe glided down the current, amid the wild and beautiful scenery of the Highlands, and along the park-like shades of a more level country. There was something in the sublime and lofty handiwork of God which fell soothingly on the sad heart of the Indian. Her thoughts were continually dwelling on the words of her dead husband, ever picturing to themselves the land of spirits where he had promised that she should join him. The perpetual change of scenery, the sunshine playing with the foliage, and the dark, heavy masses of shadow, flung from the forests and rocks on either hand, were continually exciting her untamed imagination to comparison with the heaven of her wild fancy. It seemed, at times, as if she had but to close her eyes and open them again to be in the presence of her lost one. There was something heavenly in the solemn, perpetual flow of the river, and in the music of the leaves as they rippled to the wind, that went to the poor widow's heart like the soft voice of a friend. After a day or two, the gloom which hung about her young brow, partially departed. Her cheek again dimpled to the happy laugh of her child, and when he nestled down to sleep in the furs at the bottom of the canoe, her soft, plaintive lullaby would steal over the waters like the song of a wild bird seeking in vain for its mate.

Malaeska never went on shore, except to gather wild fruit, and occasionally to kill a bird, which her true arrow seldom failed to bring down. She would strike a fire and prepare her game in some shady nook by the river side, while the canoe swung at its mooring, and her child played on the fresh grass, shouting at the cloud of summer insects that flashed by, and clapping his tiny hands at the humming-birds that came to rifle honey from the flowers that surrounded him.

The voyage was one of strange happiness to the widowed Indian. Never did Christian believe in the pages of Divine Writ with more of trust, than she placed in the dying promise of her husband, that she should meet him again in another world. His spirit seemed forever about her, and to her wild, free imagination, the passage down the magnificent stream seemed a material and glorious path to the white man's heaven. Filled with strange, sweet thoughts, she looked abroad on the mountains looming up from the banks of the river—on the forest-trees so various in their tints and so richly clothed, till she was inspired almost to forgetfulness of her affliction. She was young and healthy, and everything about her was so lovely, so grand and changing, that her heart expanded to the sunshine like a flower which has been bowed down, but not crushed beneath the force of a storm. Part of each day she spent in a wild, dreamy state of imagination. Her mind was lulled to sweet musings by the gentle sounds that hovered in the air from morning till evening; and through the long night, when all was hushed save the deep flow of the river. Birds came out with their cheerful voices at dawn, and at midday she floated in the cool shadow of the hills, or shot into some cove for a few hours' rest. When the sunset shed its gorgeous dyes over the river and the mountain ramparts, on either side, were crimson as with the track of contending armies—when the boy was asleep, and the silent stars came out to kindle up her night path, then a clear, bold melody gushed from the mother's lips like a song from the heart of a nightingale. Her eye kindled, her cheek grew warm, the dip of her paddle kept a liquid accompaniment to her rich, wild voice, as the canoe floated downward on waves that seemed rippling over a world of crushed blossoms, and were misty with the approach of evening.

Malaeska had been out many days, when the sharp gables and the tall chimneys of Manhattan broke upon her view, surrounded by the sheen of its broad bay, and by the forest which covered the uninhabited part of the island. The poor Indian gazed upon it with an unstable but troublesome fear. She urged her canoe into a little cove on the Hoboken shore, and her heart grew heavy as the grave, as she pondered on the means of fulfilling her charge. She took the letter from her bosom; the tears started to her eyes, and she kissed it with a regretful sorrow, as if a friend were about to be rendered up from her affections forever. She took the child to her heart, and held him there till its throbbings grew audible, and the strength of her misgivings could not be restrained. After a time she became more calm. She lifted the child from her bosom, laved his hands and face in the stream, and brushed his black hair with her palm till it glowed like the neck of a raven. Then she girded his little crimson robe with a string of wampum, and after arranging her own attire, shot the canoe out of the cove and urged it slowly across the mouth of the river. Her eyes were full of tears all the way, and when the child murmured, and strove to comfort her with his infant caress, she sobbed aloud, and rowed steadily forward.

It was a strange sight to the phlegmatic inhabitants of Manhattan, when Malaeska passed through their streets in full costume, and with the proud, free tread of her race. Her hair hung in long braids down her back, each braid fastened at the end with a tuft of scarlet feathers. A coronet of the same bright plumage circled her small head, and her robe was gorgeous with beads, and fringed with porcupine quills. A bow of exquisite workmanship was in her hand, and a scarf of scarlet cloth bound the boy to her back. Nothing could be more strikingly beautiful than the child. His spirited head was continually turning from one strange object to another, and his bright, black eyes were brim-full of childish wonder. One little arm was flung around his young mother's neck, and its fellow rested on the feathered arrow-shafts which crowded the quiver slung against her left shoulder. The timid, anxious look of the mother, was in strong contrast with the eager gaze of the boy. She had caught much of the delicacy and refinement of civilized life from her husband, and her manner became startled and fawn-like beneath the rude gaze of the passers-by. The modest blood burned in her cheek, and the sweet, broken English trembled on her lips, when several persons, to whom she showed the letter passed by without answering her. She did not know that they were of another nation than her husband, and spoke another language than that which love had taught her. At length she accosted an aged man who could comprehend her imperfect language. He read the name on the letter, and saw that it was addressed to his master, John Danforth, the richest fur-trader in Manhattan. The old serving-man led the way to a large, irregular building, in the vicinity of what is now Hanover Square. Malaeska followed with a lighter tread, and a heart relieved of its fear. She felt that she had found a friend in the kind old man who was conducting her to the home of her husband's father.

The servant entered this dwelling and led the way to a low parlor, paneled with oak and lighted with small panes of thick, greenish glass. A series of Dutch tiles—some of them most exquisite in finish and design, surrounded the fire-place, and a coat-of-arms, elaborately carved in oak, stood out in strong relief from the paneling above. A carpet, at that time an uncommon luxury, covered a greater portion of the floor, and the furniture was rich in its material and ponderous with heavy carved work. A tall, and rather hard-featured man sat in an arm-chair by one of the narrow windows, reading a file of papers which had just arrived in the last merchant-ship from London. A little distance from him, a slight and very thin lady of about fifty was occupied with household sewing; her work-box stood on a small table before her, and a book of common-prayer lay beside it. The servant had intended to announce his strange guest, but, fearful of losing sight of him, Malaeska followed close upon his footsteps, and before he was aware of it, stood within the room, holding her child by the hand.

"A woman, sir,—an Indian woman, with a letter," said the embarrassed servant, motioning his charge to draw back. But Malaeska had stepped close to the merchant, and was looking earnestly in his face when he raised his eyes from the papers. There was something cold in his severe gaze as he fixed it on her through his spectacles. The Indian felt chilled and repulsed; her heart was full, and she turned with a look of touching appeal to the lady. That face was one to which a child would have fled for comfort; it was tranquil and full of kindness. Malaeska's face brightened as she went up to her, and placed the letter in her hands without speaking a word; but the palpitation of her heart was visible through her heavy garments, and her hands shook as she relinquished the precious paper.

"The seal is black," said the lady, turning very pale as she gave the letter to her husband, "but it is *his* writing," she added, with a forced smile. "He could not have sent word himself, were he—ill." She hesitated at the last word, for, spite of herself, the thoughts of death lay heavily at her heart.

The merchant composed himself in his chair, settled his spectacles, and after another severe glance at the bearer, opened the letter. His wife kept her eyes fixed anxiously on his face as he read. She saw that his face grew pale, that his high, narrow forehead contracted, and that the stern mouth became still more rigid in its expression. She knew that some evil had befallen her son—her only son, and she grasped a chair for support; her lips were bloodless, and her eyes became keen with agonizing suspense. When her husband had read the letter through, she went close to him, but looked another way as she spoke.

"Tell me! has any harm befallen my son?" Her voice was low and gentle, but with husky suspense.

Her husband did not answer, but his hand fell heavily upon his knee, and the letter rattled in his unsteady grasp, his eyes were fixed on his trembling wife with a look that chilled her to the heart. She attempted to withdraw the letter from his hand, but he clenched it the firmer.

22

"Let it alone—he is dead—murdered by the savages—why should you know more?"

The poor woman staggered back, and the fire of anxiety went out from her eyes.

"Can there be any thing worse than death—the death of the first-born of our youth—cut off in his proud manhood?" she murmured, in a low, broken voice.

"Yes, woman!" said the husband, almost fiercely; "there is a thing worse than death—disgrace!"

"Disgrace coupled with my son? You are his father, John. Do not slander him now that he is dead—before his mother, too." There was a faint, red spot then upon that mild woman's face, and her mouth curved proudly as she spoke. All that was stern in her nature had been aroused by the implied charge against the departed.

"Read, woman, read! Look on that accursed wretch and her child! They have enticed him into their savage haunts, and murdered him. Now they come to claim protection and reward for the foul deed."

Malaeska drew her child closer to her as she listened to this vehement language, and shrank slowly back to a corner of the room, where she crouched, like a frightened hare, looking wildly about, as if seeking some means to evade the vengeance which seemed to threaten her.

After the first storm of feeling, the old man buried his face in his hands and remained motionless, while the sobs of his wife, as she read her son's letter, alone broke the stillness of the room.

Malaeska felt those tears as an encouragement, and her own deep feelings taught her how to reach those of another. She drew timidly to the mourner and sank at her feet.

"Will the white woman look upon Malaeska?" she said, in a voice full of humility and touching earnestness. "She loved the young white chief, and when the shadows fell upon his soul, he said that his mother's heart would grow soft to the poor Indian woman who had slept in his bosom while she was very young. He said that her love would open to his boy like a flower to the sunshine. Will the white woman look upon the boy? He is like his father."

"He is, poor child, he is!" murmured the bereaved mother, looking on the boy through her tears—"like him, as he was when we were both young, and he the blessing of our hearts. Oh, John, do you remember his smile?—how his cheek would dimple when we kissed it! Look upon this poor, fatherless creature; they are all here again; the sunny eye and the broad forehead. Look upon him, John, for my sake—for the sake of our dead son, who prayed us with his last breath to love *his* son. Look upon him!"

The kind woman led the child to her husband as she spoke, and resting her arm on his shoulder, pressed her lips upon his swollen temples. The pride of his nature was touched. His bosom heaved, and tears gushed through his rigid fingers. He felt a little form draw close to his knee, and a tiny, soft hand strive with its feeble might to uncover his face. The voice of nature was strong within him. His hands dropped, and he pored with a troubled face over the uplifted features of the child.

Tears were in those young, bright eyes as they returned his grandfather's gaze, but when a softer expression came into the old man's face, a smile broke through them, and the little fellow lifted both his arms and clasped them over the bowed neck of his grandfather. There was a momentary struggle, and then the merchant folded the boy to his heart with a burst of strong feeling such as his iron nature had seldom known.

"He *is* like his father. Let the woman go back to her tribe; we will keep the boy."

Malaeska sprang forward, clasped her hands, and turned with an air of wild, heart-thrilling appeal to the lady.

"You will not send Malaeska from her child. No—no, white woman. Your boy has slept against your heart, and you have felt his voice in your ear, like the song of a young mocking-bird. You would not send the poor Indian back to the woods without her child. She has come to you from the forest, that she may learn the path to the white man's heaven, and see her husband again, and you will not show it her. Give the Indian woman her boy; her heart is growing very strong; she will not go back to the woods alone!"

As she spoke these words, with an air more energetic even than her speech, she snatched the child from his grandfather's arms, and stood like a lioness guarding her young, her lips writhing and her black eyes flashing fire, for the savage blood kindled in her veins at the thought of being separated from her son.

"Be quiet, girl, be quiet. If you go, the child shall go with you," said the gentle Mrs. Danforth. "Do not give way to this fiery spirit; no one will wrong you."

Malaeska dropped her air of defiance, and placing the child humbly at his grandfather's feet, drew back, and stood with her eyes cast down, and her hands clasped deprecatingly together, a posture of supplication in strong contrast with her late wild demeanor.

"Let them stay. Do not separate the mother and the child!" entreated the kind lady, anxious to soothe away the effect of her husband's violence. "The thoughts of a separation drives her wild, poor thing. *He* loved her;—why should we send her back to her savage haunts? Read this letter once more, my husband. You can not refuse the dying request of our first-born."

With gentle and persuasive words like these, the kind lady prevailed. Malaeska was allowed to remain in the house of her husband's father, but it was only as the nurse of her own son. She was not permitted to acknowledge herself as his mother; and it was given out that young Danforth had married in one of the new settlements—that the young couple had fallen victims to the savages, and that their infant son had been rescued by an Indian girl, who brought him to his grandfather. The story easily gained credit, and it was no matter of wonder that the old fur merchant soon became fondly attached to the little orphan, or that the preserver of his grandchild was made an object of grateful attention in his household.

CHAPTER IV.

"Her heart is in the wild wood; Her heart is not here. Her heart is in the wild wood; It was hunting the deer."

It would have been an unnatural thing had that picturesque young mother abandoned the woods, and prisoned herself in a quaint old Dutch house, under the best circumstances. The wild bird which has fluttered freely from its nest through a thousand forests, might as well be expected to love its cage, as this poor wild girl her new home, with its dreary stillness and its leaden regularity. But love was all-powerful in that wild heart. It had brought Malaeska from her forest home, separated her from her tribe in its hour of bitter defeat, and sent her a forlorn wanderer among strangers that regarded her almost with loathing.

The elder Danforth was a just man, but hard as granite in his prejudices. An only son had been murdered by the savages to whom this poor young creature belonged. His blood—all of his being that might descend to posterity—had been mingled with the accursed race who had sacrificed him. Gladly would he have rent the two races asunder, in the very person of his grandchild, could the pure half of his being been thus preserved,

But he was a proud, childish old man, and there was something in the boy's eyes, in the brave lift of his head, and in his caressing manner, which filled the void in his heart, half with love and half with pain. He could no more separate the two passions in his own soul, than he could drain the savage blood from the little boy's veins.

But the house-mother, the gentle wife, could see nothing but her son's smile in that young face, nothing but his look in the large eyes, which, black in color, still possessed something of the azure light that had distinguished those of the father.

The boy was more cheerful and bird-like than his mother, for all her youth had gone out on the banks of the pond where her husband died. Always submissive, always gentle, she was nevertheless a melancholy woman. A bird which had followed its young out into strange lands, and caged it there, could not have hovered around it more hopelessly.

Nothing but her husband's dying wish would have kept Malaeska in Manhattan. She thought of her own people incessantly—of her broken, harassed tribe, desolated by the death of her father, and whose young chief she had carried off and given to strangers.

But shame dyed Malaeska's cheek as she thought of these things. What right had she, an Indian of the pure blood, to bring the grandchild of her father under the roof of his enemies? Why had she not taken the child in her arms and joined her people as they sang the death-chant for her father, "who," she murmured to herself again and again, "was a great chief," and retreated with them deep into the wilderness, to which they were driven, giving them a chief in her son?

But no! passion had been too strong in Malaeska's heart. The woman conquered the patriot; and the refinement which affection had given her, enslaved the wild nature without returning a compensation of love for the sacrifice. She pined for her people—all the more that they were in peril and sorrow. She longed for the shaded forest-path, and the pretty lodge, with its couches of fur and its floor of blossoming turf. To her the very winds seemed chained among the city houses; and when she heard them sighing through the gables, it seemed to her that they were moaning for freedom, as she was in the solitude of her lonely life.

They had taken the child from her. A white nurse was found who stepped in between the young heir and his mother, thrusting her ruthlessly aside. In this the old man was obstinate. The wild blood of the boy must be quenched; he must know nothing of the race from which his disgrace sprang. If the Indian woman remained under his roof, it must be as a menial, and on condition that all natural affection lay crushed within her—unexpressed, unguessed at by the household.

But Mrs. Danforth had compassion on the poor mother. She remembered the time when her own child made all the pulses of her being thrill with love, which now took the form of a thousand tender regrets. She could not watch the lone Indian stealing off to her solitary room under the gable roof—a mother, yet childless—without throbs of womanly sorrow. She was far too good a wife to brave her husband's authority, but, with the cowardliness of a kind heart, she frequently managed to evade it. Sometimes in the night she would creep out of her prim chamber, and steal the boy from the side of his nurse, whom she bore on her own motherly bosom to the solitary bed of Malaeska.

As if Malaeska had a premonition of the kindliness, she was sure to be wide awake, thinking of her child, and ready to gush forth in murmurs of thankfulness for the joy of clasping her own son a moment to that lonely heart.

Then the grandmother would steal to her husband's side again, charging it upon her memory to awake before daylight, and carry the boy back to the stranger's bed, making her gentle charity a secret as if it had been a sin.

It was pitiful to see Malaeska haunting the footsteps of her boy all the day long. If he was taken into the garden, she was sure to be hovering around the old pear-trees, where she could sometimes unseen lure him from his play, and lavish kisses on his mouth as he laughed recklessly, and strove to abandon her for some bright flower or butterfly that crossed his path. This snatch of affection, this stealthy way of appeasing a hungry nature, was enough to drive a well-tutored woman mad; as for Malaeska, it was a marvel that she could tame her erratic nature into the abject position allotted her in that family. She had neither the occupation of a servant, nor the interests of an equal.

Forbidden to associate with the people in the kitchen, yet never welcomed in the formal parlor when its master was at home, she hovered around the halls and corners of the house, or hid herself away in the gable chambers, embroidering beautiful trifles on scraps of silk and fragments of bright cloth, with which she strove to bribe the woman who controlled her child, into forbearance and kindness.

But alas, poor woman! submission to the wishes of the dead was a terrible duty; her poor heart was breaking all the time; she had no hope, no life; the very glance of her eye was an appeal for mercy; her step, as it fell on the turf, was laden with despondency—she had nothing on earth to live for.

This state of things arose when the child was a little boy; but as he grew older the bitterness of Malaeska's lot became more intense. The nurse who had supplanted her went away; for he was becoming a fine lad, and far removed from the need of woman's care. But this brought her no nearer to his affections. The Indian blood was strong in his young veins; he loved such play as brought activity and danger with it, and broke from the Indian woman's caresses with a sort of scorn, and she knew that the old grandfather's prejudice was taking root in his heart, and dared not utter a protest. She was forbidden to lavish tenderness on her son, or to call forth his in return, lest it might create suspicion of the relationship.

In his early boyhood, she could steal to his chamber at night, and give free indulgence to the wild tenderness of her nature; but after a time even the privilege of watching him in his sleep was denied to her. Once, when she broke the tired boy's rest by her caresses, he became petulant, and eluded her for her obtrusiveness. The repulse went to her heart like iron. She had no power to plead; for her life, she dared not tell him the secret of that aching love which she felt—too cruelly felt—oppressed his boyhood; for that would be to expose the disgrace of blood which embittered the old man's pride.

She was his mother; yet her very existence in that house was held as a reproach. Every look that she dared to cast on her child, was watched jealously as a fault. Poor Malaeska! hers was a sad, sad life.

She had borne every thing for years, dreaming, poor thing, that the eternal cry that went up from her heart would be answered, as the boy grew older; but when he began to shrink proudly from her caresses, and question the love that was killing her, the despair which smoldered at her heart broke forth, and the forest blood spoke out with a power that not even a sacred memory of the dead could oppose. A wild idea seized upon her. She would no longer remain in the white man's house, like a bird beating its wings against the wires of a cage. The forests were wide and green as ever. Her people might yet be found. She would seek them in the wilderness. The boy should go with her, and become the chief of his tribe, as her father had been. That old man should not forever trample down her heart. There was a free life which she would find or die.

The boy's childish petulance had created this wild wish in his mother's heart. The least sign of repulsion drove her frantic. She began to thirst eagerly for her old free existence in the woods; but for the blood of her husband, which ran in the old man's veins, she would have given way to the savage hate of her people, against the household in which she had been so unhappy. As it was, she only panted to be away with her child, who must love her when no white man stood by to rebuke him. With her aroused energies the native reticence of her tribe came to her aid. The stealthy art of warfare against an enemy awoke. They should not know how wretched she was. Her plans must be securely made. Every step toward freedom should be carefully considered. These thoughts occupied Malaeska for days and weeks. She became active in her little chamber. The bow and sheaf of arrows that had given her the appearance of a young Diana when she came to Manhattan in her canoe, were taken down from the wall, newly strung, and the stone arrow-heads patiently sharpened. Her dress, with its gorgeous embroidery of fringe and wampum, was examined with care. She must return to her people as she had left them. The daughter of a chief—the mother of a chief—not a fragment of the white man's bounty should go with her to the forest.

Cautiously, and with something of native craft, Malaeska made her preparations. Down upon the shores of the Hudson, lived an old carpenter who made boats for a living. Malaeska had often seen him at his work, and her rude knowledge of his craft gave peculiar interest to the curiosity with which she regarded him. The Indian girl had long been an object of his especial interest, and the carpenter was flattered by her admiration of his work.

One day she came to his house with a look of eager watchfulness. Her step was hurried, her eye wild as a hawk's when its prey is near. The old man was finishing a fanciful little craft, of which he was proud beyond any thing. It was so light, so strong, so beautifully decorated with bands of red and white around the edge—no wonder the young woman's eyes brightened when she saw it.

"What would he take for the boat?" That was a droll question from her. Why, he had built it to please his own fancy. A pair of oars would make it skim the water like a bird. He had built it with an eye to old Mr. Danforth, who had been down to look at his boats for that dark-eyed grandson, whom he seemed to worship. None of his boats were fanciful or light enough for the lad. So he had built this at a venture.

Malaeska's eyes kindled brighter and brighter. Yes, yes; she, too, was thinking of the young gentleman; she would bring him to look at the boat. Mrs. Danforth often trusted the boy out with her; if he would only tell the price, perhaps they might be able to bring the money, and give the boat a trial on the Hudson.

The old man laughed, glanced proudly at his handiwork, and named a price. It was not too much; Malaeska had double that amount in the embroidered pouch that hung in her little room at home—for the old gentleman had been liberal to her in every thing but kindness. She went home elated and eager; all was in readiness. The next day—oh, how her heart glowed as she thought of the next day!

CHAPTER V.

Her boat is on the river, With the boy by her side; With her bow and her quiver She stands in her pride.

The next afternoon old Mr. Danforth was absent from home. A municipal meeting, or something of that kind, was to be attended, and he was always prompt in the performance of public duties. The good housewife had not been well for some days. Malaeska, always a gentle nurse, attended her with unusual assiduity. There was something evidently at work in the Indian woman's heart. Her lips were pale, her eyes full of pathetic trouble. After a time, when weariness made the old lady sleepy, Malaeska stole to the bedside, and kneeling down, kissed the withered hand that fell over the bed, with strange humility. This action was so light that the good lady did not heed it, but afterward it came to her like a dream, and as such she remembered this leave-taking of the poor mother.

William—for the lad was named after his father—was in a moody state that afternoon. He had no playfellows, for the indisposition of his grandmother had shut all strangers from the house, so he went into the garden, and began to draw the outlines of a rude fortification from the white pebbles that paved the principal walk. He was interrupted in the work by a pair of orioles, that came dashing through the leaves of an old apple-tree in a far end of the garden, in full chase and pursuit, making the very air vibrate with their rapid motion.

After chasing each other up and down, to and fro in the clear sunshine, they were attracted by something in the distance, and darted off like a couple of golden arrows, sending back wild gushes of music in the start.

The boy had been watching them with his great eyes full of envious delight. Their riotous freedom charmed him; he felt chained and caged even in that spacious garden, full of golden fruit and bright flowers as it was. The native fire kindled in his frame.

"Oh, if I were only a bird, that could fly home when I pleased and away to the woods again—the bright, beautiful woods that can see across the river, but never must play in. How the bird must love it though!"

The boy stopped speaking, for, like any other child kept to himself he was talking over his thoughts aloud. But a shadow fell across the white pebbles on which he sat, and this it was which disturbed him.

It was the Indian woman, Malaeska, with a forced smile on her face and looking wildly strange. She seemed larger and more stately than when he had seen her last. In her hand she held a light bow tufted with yellow and crimson feathers. When she saw his eyes brighten at the sight of the bow, Malaeska took an arrow from the sheaf which she carried under her cloak, and fitted it to the string.

"See, this is what we learn in the woods."

The two birds were wheeling to and fro across the garden and out into the open space; their plumage flashed in the sunshine and gushes of musical triumph floated back as one shot ahead of the other. Malaeska lifted her bow with something of her old forest gracefulness—a faint twang of the bowstring—a sharp whiz of the arrow, and one of the birds fluttered downward, with a sad little cry, and fell upon the ground, trembling like a broken poplar flower.

The boy started up—his eye brightened and his thin nostrils dilated, the savage instincts of his nature broke out in all his features.

"And you learned to do this in the woods, Malaeska?" he said, eagerly.

"Yes; will you learn too?"

"Oh, yes—give hold here—quick—quick!"

"Not here; we learn these things in the woods; come with me, and I will show you all about it."

Malaeska grew pale as she spoke, and trembled in all her limbs. What if the boy refused to go with her?

"What! over the river to the woods that look so bright and so brown when the nuts fall? Will you take me there, Malaeska?"

"Yes, over the river where it shines like silver."

"You will? oh my!—but how?"

28

"Hush! not so loud. In a beautiful little boat."

"With white sails, Malaeska?"

"No—with paddles."

"Ah, me!—but I can't make them go in the water; once grandfather let me try, but I had to give it up."

"But I can make them go."

"You! why, that isn't a woman's work."

"No, but everybody learns it in the woods."

"Can I?"

"Yes!"

"Then come along before grandfather comes to say we shan't; come along, I say; I want to shoot and run and live in the woods—come along Malaeska. Quick, or somebody will shut the gate."

Malaeska looked warily around—on the windows of the house, through the thickets, and along the gravel walks. No one was in sight. She and her boy were all alone. She breathed heavily and lingered, thinking of the poor lady within.

"Come!" cried the boy, eagerly; "I want to go—come along to the woods."

"Yes, yes," whispered Malaeska, "to the woods—it is our home. There I shall be a mother once more."

With the steps of a young deer, starting for its covert, she left the garden. The boy kept bravely on with her, bounding forward with a laugh when her step was too rapid for him to keep up with it. Thus, in breathless haste, they passed through the town into the open country and along the rough banks of the river.

A little inlet, worn by the constant action of the water, ran up into the shore, which is now broken with wharves and bristling with masts. A clump of old forest-hemlocks bent over the waters, casting cool, green shadows upon it till the sun was far in the west.

In these shadows, rocking sleepily on the ripples, lay the pretty boat which Malaeska had purchased. A painted basket, such as the peaceful Indians sometimes sent to market, stood in the stern stored with bread; a tiger skin edged with crimson cloth, according to the Indian woman's fancy, lay along the bottom of the boat, and cushions of scarlet cloth, edged with an embroidery of beads, lay on the seat.

William Danforth broke into a shout when he saw the boat and its appointments.

"Are we going in this? May I learn to row, now—now?" With a leap he sprang into the little craft, and seizing the oars, called out for her to come on, for he was in a hurry to begin.

Malaeska loosened the cable, and holding the end in her hand, sprang to the side of her child.

"Not yet, my chief, not yet; give the oars to me a little while; when we can no longer see the steeples, you shall pull them," she said.

The boy gave up his place with an impatient toss of his head, which sent the black curls flying over his temples. But the boat shot out into the river with a velocity that took away his breath, and he sat down in the bow, laughing as the silver spray rained over him. With her face to the north, and her eyes flashing with the eager joy of escape, Malaeska dashed up the river; every plunge of the oars was a step toward freedom—every gleam of the sun struck her as a smile from the Great Spirit to whom her husband and father had gone.

When the sun went down, and the twilight came on, the little boat was far up the river. It had glided under the shadows of Weehawken, and was skirting the western shore toward the Highlands, at that time crowned by an unbroken forest, and savage in the grandeur of wild nature.

Now Malaeska listened to the entreaties of her boy, and gave the oars into his small hands. No matter though the boat receded under his brave but imperfect efforts; once out of sight of the town, Malaeska had less fear, and smiled securely at the energy with which the little fellow beat the waters. He was indignant if she attempted to help him, and the next moment was sure to send a storm of rain over her in some more desperate effort to prove how capable he was of taking the labor from her hands.

Thus the night came on, soft and calm, wrapping the mother and child in a world of silvery moonbeams. The shadows which lay along the hills bounded their watery path with gloom. This made the boy sad, and he began to feel mournfully weary; but scenes like this were familiar with Malaeska, and her old nature rose high and free in this solitude which included all that she had in the living world—her freedom and the son of her white husband.

"Malaeska," said the boy, creeping to her side, and laying his head on her lap, "Malaeska, I am tired—I want to go home."

"Home! but you have not seen the woods. Courage, my chief, and we will go on ashore."

"But it is black—so black, and something is crying there—something that is sick or wants to get home like me."

"No, no,—it is only a whippowil singing to the night."

"A whippowil? Is that a little boy, Malaeska? Let us bring him into the boat."

"No, my child, it is only a bird."

"Poor bird!" sighed the boy; "how it wants to get home."

"No, it loves the woods. The bird would die if you took it from the shade of the trees," said Malaeska, striving to pacify the boy, who crept upward into her lap and laid his cheek against hers. She felt that he trembled, and that tears lay cold on his cheeks. "Don't, my William, but look up and see how many stars hang over us—the river is full of them."

"Oh, but grandfather will be missing me," pleaded the boy. Malaeska felt herself chilled; she had taken the boy but not his memory; that went back to the opulent home he had left. With her at his side, and the beautiful universe around, he thought of the old man who had made her worse than a serf in his household—who had stolen away the human soul that God had given into her charge. The Indian woman grew sad to the very depths of her soul when the boy spoke of his grandfather.

"Come," she said with mournful pathos, "now we will find an open place in the woods. You shall have a bed like the pretty flowers. I will build a fire, and you shall see it grow red among the branches."

The boy smiled in the moonlight.

"A fire out of doors! Yes, yes, let's go into the woods. Will the birds talk to us there?"

"The birds talk to us always when we get into the deep of the woods."

Malaeska urged her boat into a little inlet that ran up between two great rocks upon the shore, where it was sheltered and safe; then she took the tiger-skin and the cushions in her arms, and, cautioning the boy to hold on to her dress, began to mount a little elevation where the trees were thin and the grass abundant, as she could tell from the odor of wild-flowers that came with the wind. A rock lay embedded in this rich forest-grass, and over it a huge white poplar spread its branches like a tent.

Upon this rock Malaeska enthroned the boy, talking to him all the time, as she struck sparks from a flint which she took from her basket, and began to kindle a fire from the dry sticks which lay around in abundance. When William saw the flames rise up high and clear, illuminating the beautiful space around, and shooting gleams of gold through the poplar's branches, he grew brave again, and coming down from his eminence, began to gather brushwood that the fire might keep bright. Then Malaeska took a bottle of water and some bread, with fragments of dried beef, from her basket, and the boy came smiling from his work. He was no longer depressed by the dark, and the sight of food made him hungry.

How proudly the Indian mother broke the food and surrendered it to his eager appetite. The bright beauty of her face was something wonderful to look upon as she watched him by the firelight. For the first time, since he was a little infant, he really seemed to belong to her.

When he was satisfied with food, and she saw that his eyelids began to droop, Malaeska went to some rocks a little distance, and tearing up the moss in great green fleeces, brought it to the place she had chosen under the poplar-tree, and heaped a soft couch for the child. Over this she spread the tiger-skin with its red border, and laid the crimson pillows whose fringes glittered in the firelight like gems around the couch of a prince.

To this picturesque bed Malaeska took the boy, and seating herself by his side, began to sing as she had done years ago under the roof of her wigwam. The lad was very weary, and fell asleep while her plaintive voice filled the air and was answered mournfully back by a night-bird deep in the blackness of the forest.

When certain that the lad was asleep, Malaeska lay down on the hard rock by his side, softly stealing one arm over him and sighing out her troubled joy as she pressed his lips with her timid kisses.

Thus the poor Indian sunk to a broken rest, as she had done all her life, piling up soft couches for those she loved, and taking the cold stone for herself. It was her woman's destiny, not the more certain because of her savage origin. Civilization does not always reverse this mournful picture of womanly self-abnegation.

When the morning came, the boy was aroused by a full chorus of singing-birds that fairly made the air vibrate with their melody. In and out through the branches ran their wild minstrelsy, till the sunshine laughing through the greenness, giving warmth and pleasant light to the music. William sat up, rubbing his eyes, and wondering at the strange noises. Then he remembered where he was, called aloud for Malaeska. She came from behind a clump of trees, carrying a patridge in her hand, pierced through the heart with her arrow. She flung the bird on the rock at William's feet, and kneeling down before him, kissed his feet, his hands, and the folds of his tunic, smoothing his hair and his garments with pathetic fondness.

"When shall we go home, Malaeska?" cried the lad, a little anxiously. "Grandfather will want us."

"This is the home for a young chief," replied the mother, looking around upon the pleasant sky and the forest-turf, enameled with wild-flowers. "What white man has a tent like this?"

The boy looked up and saw a world of golden tulip-blossoms starring the branches above him.

"It lets in the cold and the rain," he said, shaking the dew from his glossy hair. "I don't like the woods, Malaeska."

"But you will—oh yes, you will," answered the mother, with anxious cheerfulness; "see, I have shot a bird for your breakfast."

"A bird; and I am so hungry."

"And see here, what I have brought from the shore."

She took a little leaf-basket from a recess in the rocks, and held it up full of black raspberries with the dew glittering upon them.

The boy clapped his hands, laughing merrily.

"Give me the raspberries—I will eat them all. Grandfather isn't here to stop me, so I will eat and eat till the basket is empty. After all, Malaeska, it is pleasant being in the woods—come, pour the berries on the moss, just here, and get another basketful while I eat these; but don't go far—I am afraid when you are out of sight. No, no, let me build the fire—see how I can make the sparks fly."

Down he came from the rock, forgetting his berries, and eager to distinguish himself among the brushwood, while Malaeska withdrew a little distance and prepared her game for roasting.

The boy was quick and full of intelligence; he had a fire blazing at once, and shouted back a challenge to the birds as its flames rose in the air, sending up wreaths of delicate blue smoke into the poplar branches, and curtaining the rocks with mist.

Directly the Indian woman came forward with her game, nicely dressed and pierced with a wooden skewer; to this she attached a piece of twine, which, being tied to a branch overhead, swung its burden to and fro before the fire.

While this rustic breakfast was in preparation, the boy went off in search of flowers or berries—any thing that he could find. He came back with a quantity of green wild cherries in his tunic, and a bird's nest, with three speckled eggs in it, which he had found under a tuft of fern leaves. A striped squirrel, that ran down a chestnut-limb, looked at him with such queer earnestness, that he shouted lustily to Malaeska, saying that he loved the beautiful woods and all the pretty things in it.

When he came back, Malaeska had thrown off her cloak, and crowned herself with a coronal of scarlet and green feathers, which rendered her savage dress complete, and made her an object of wondering admiration to the boy, as she moved in and out through the trees, with her face all aglow with proud love.

While the patridge was swaying to and fro before the fire, Malaeska gathered a handful of chestnut-leaves and wove them together in a sort of mat; upon this cool nest she laid the bird, and carved it with a pretty poniard which William's father had given her in his first wooing; then she made a leaf-cup, and, going to a little spring which she had discovered, filled it with crystal water. So, upon the flowering turf, with wild birds serenading them, and the winds floating softly by, the mother and boy took their first regular meal in the forest. William was delighted; every thing was fresh and beautiful to him. He could scarcely contain his eagerness to be in action long enough to eat the delicate repast which Malaeska diversified with smiles and caresses. He wanted to shoot the birds that sang so sweetly in the branches, all unconscious that the act would inflict pain on the poor little songsters, he could not satisfy himself with gazing on the gorgeous raiment of his mother—it was something wonderful in his eyes.

At last the rustic meal was ended, and, with his lips reddened by the juicy fruit, he started up, pleading for the bow and arrow.

Proud as a queen and fond as a woman, Malaeska taught him how to place the arrow on the bowstring, and when to lift it gradually toward his face. He took to it naturally, the young rogue, and absolutely danced for joy when his first arrow leaped from his bow and went rifling through the poplar leaves. How Malaeska loved this practice! how she triumphed in each graceful lift of his arm! how her heart leaped to the rich tumult of his shouts! He wanted to go off alone and try his skill among the squirrels, but Malaeska was afraid, and followed him step by step, happy and watchful. Every moment increased his skill; he would have exhausted the sheaf of arrows, but that Malaeska patiently searched for them after each shot, and thus secured constant amusement till he grew tired even of that rare sport.

Toward noon, Malaeska left him at rest on the tiger-skin, and went herself in search of game for the noonday meal; never had she breathed so freely; never had the woods seemed so like her home. A sense of profound peace stole over her. These groves were her world, and on the rock near by lay her other life—all that she had on earth to love. She was in no haste to find her tribe. What care had she for any thing while the boy was with her, and the forest so pleasant! What did she care for but his happiness?

It required but few efforts of her woodcraft to obtain game enough for another pleasant meal; so, with a light step, she returned to her fairy-like encampment. Tired with his play, the boy had fallen asleep on the rock. She saw the graceful repose of his limbs, and the sunshine shimmering softly through his black hair. Her step grew lighter; she was afraid of rustling a leaf, lest the noise might disturb him. Thus, softly and almost holding her breath, she drew nearer and nearer to the rock. All at once a faint gasping breath bespoke some terrible emotion—she stood motionless, rooted to the earth. A low rattle checked her first, and then she saw the shimmer of a serpent, coiled upon the very rock where her boy was lying. Her approach had aroused the reptile, and she could see him preparing to lance out. His first fling would be at the sleeping boy. The mother was frozen into marble; she dared not move—she could only stare at the snake with a wild glitter of the eye.

The stillness seemed to appease the creature. The noise of his rattle grew fainter, and his eyes sank like waning fire-sparks into the writhing folds that settled on the moss. But the child was disturbed by a sunbeam that slanted through the leaves overhead, and turned upon the tiger-skin. Instantly the rattle sounded sharp and clear, and out from the writhing folds shot the venomous head with its vicious eyes fixed on the boy. Malaeska had, even in her frozen state, some thought of saving her boy. With her cold hands she had fitted the arrow and lifted the bow, but as the serpent grew passive, the weapon dropped again; for he lay on the other side of the child, and to kill him she was obliged to shoot over that sleeping form. But the reptile crested himself again, and now with a quiver of horrible dread at her heart, but nerves strained like steel, she drew the bowstring, and, aiming at the head which glittered like a jewel, just beyond her child, let the arrow fly. She went blind on the instant—the darkness of death fell upon her brain; the coldness of death lay upon her heart; she listened for some cry—nothing but a sharp rustling of leaves and then profound stillness met her strained senses.

The time in which Malaeska was struck with darkness seemed an eternity to her, but it lasted only an instant, in fact; then her eyes opened wide in the agonized search, and terrible thrills shot through her frame. A laugh rang up through the trees, and then she saw her boy sitting up on the tiger-skin, his cheeks all rosy with sleep and dimpled with surprise, gazing down upon the headless rattlesnake that had uncoiled convulsively in its death-spasms, and lay quivering across his feet.

"Ha! ha!" he shouted, clapping his hands, "this is a famous fellow—prettier than the birds, prettier than the squirrels. Malaeska! Malaeska! see what this checkered thing is with no head, and rings on its tail."

Malaeska was so weak she could hardly stand, but, trembling in every limb, she staggered toward the rock, and seizing upon the still quivering snake, hurled it with a shuddering cry into the undergrowth.

Then she fell upon her knees, and clasped the boy close, close to her bosom till he struggled and cried out that she was hurting him. But she could not let him go; it seemed as if the serpent would coil around him the moment her arms were loosened; she clung to his garments—she kissed his hands, his hair, and his flushed forehead with passionate energy.

He could not understand all this. Why did Malaeska breathe so hard, and shake so much? He wished she had not flung away the pretty creature which had crept to his bed while he slept, and looked so beautiful. But when she told how dangerous the reptile was, he began to be afraid and questioned her with vague terror about the way she had killed him.

Some yards from the rock, Malaeska found her arrow on which the serpent's head was impaled, and she carried it with trembling exultation to the boy, who shrank away with new-born dread, and began to know what fear was.

CHAPTER VI.

"Mid forests and meadow lands, though we may roam, Be it ever so humble, there's no place like home; Home, home, sweet, sweet home, There's no place like home; There's no place like home."

This event troubled Malaeska, and gathering up her little property, she unmoored the boat, and made progress up the river. The child was delighted with the change, and soon lost all unpleasant remembrance of the rattlesnake. But Malaeska was very careful in the selection of her encampment that afternoon, and kindled a bright fire before she spread the tiger-skin for William's bed, which she trusted would keep all venomous things away. They ate their supper under a huge white pine, that absorbed the firelight in its dusky branches, and made every thing gloomy around. As the darkness closed over them William grew silent, and by the heaviness of his features Malaeska saw that he was oppressed by thoughts of home. She had resolved not to tell him of the relationship which was constantly in her thoughts, till they should stand at the council-fires of the tribe, when the Indians should know him as their chief, and he recognize a mother in poor Malaeska.

Troubled by his sad look, the Indian woman sought for something in her stores that should cheer him. She found some seed-cakes, golden and sweet, which only brought tears into the child's eyes, for they reminded him of home and all its comforts.

"Malaeska," he said, "when shall we go back to grandfather and grandmother? I know they want to see us."

"No, no; we must not think about that," said Malaeska anxiously.

"But I can't help it—how can I?" persisted the boy, mournfully.

"Don't—don't say you love them—I mean your grandfather—more than you love Malaeska. She would die for you."

"Yes; but I don't want you to die, only to go back home," he pleaded.

"We are going home—to our beautiful home in the woods, which I told you of.

"Dear me, I'm tired of the woods."

"Tired of the woods?"

"Yes, I *am* tired. They are nice to play in, but it isn't home, no way. How far is it, Malaeska, to where grandfather lives?"

"I don't know—I don't want to know. We shall never—never go there again," said the Indian, passionately. "You are mine, all mine."

The boy struggled in her embrace, restively.

"But I won't stay in the woods. I want to be in a real house, and sleep in a soft bed, and—and—there, now, it is going to rain; I hear it thunder. Oh, how I want to go home!"

There was in truth a storm mustering over them; the wind rose and moaned hoarsely through the pines. Malaeska was greatly distressed, and gathered the tired boy lovingly to her bosom for shelter.

"Have patience, William; nothing shall hurt you. To-morrow we will row the boat all day. You shall pull the oars yourself."

"Shall I, though?" said the boy, brightening a little; "but will it be on the way home?"

"We shall go across the mountains where the Indians live. The brave warriors who will make William their king."

"But I don't want to be a king, Malaeska!"

"A chief—a great chief—who shall go to the war-path and fight battles."

"Ah, I should like that, with your pretty bow and arrow, Malaeska; wouldn't I shoot the wicked red-skins?"

"Ah, my boy, don't say that."

"Oh," said the child, shivering, "the wind is cold; how it sobs in the pine boughs. Don't you wish we were at home now?"

"Don't be afraid of the cold," said Malaeska, in a troubled voice; "see, I will wrap this cloak about you, and no rain can come through the fur blanket. We are brave, you and I— what do we care for a little thunder and rain—it makes me feel brave."

"But you don't care for home; you love the woods and the rain. The thunder and lightning makes your eyes bright, but I don't like it; so take me home, please, and then you may go to the woods; I won't tell."

"Oh, don't—don't. It breaks my heart," cried the poor mother. "Listen, William; the Indians—my people—the brave Indians want you for a chief. In a few years you shall lead them to war."

"But I hate the Indians."

"No, no."

"They are fierce and cruel."

"Not to you—not to you!"

"I won't live with the Indians!"

"They are a brave people—you shall be their chief."

"They killed my father."

"But I am of those people. I saved you and brought you among the white people."

"Yes, I know; grandmother told me that."

"And I belonged to the woods."

"Among the Indians?"

"Yes. Your father loved these Indians, William."

"Did he—but they killed him."

"But it was in battle."

"In fair battle; did you say that?"

"Yes, child. Your father was friendly with them, but they thought he had turned enemy. A great chief met him in the midst of the fight, and they killed each other. They fell and died together."

"Did you know this great chief, Malaeska."

"He was my father," answered the Indian woman, hoarsely; "my own father."

"Your father and mine; how strange that they should hate each other," said the boy, thoughtfully.

"Not always," answered Malaeska, struggling against the tears that choked her words; "at one time they loved each other."

"Loved each other! Did my father love you, Malaeska?"

White as death the poor woman turned; a hand was clenched under her deer-skin robe, and pressed hard against her heart; but she had promised to reveal nothing, and bravely kept her word.

The boy forgot his reckless question the moment it was asked, and did not heed her pale silence, for the storm was gathering darkly over them. Malaeska wrapped him in her cloak, and sheltered him with her person. The rain began to patter heavily overhead; but the pine tree was thick with foliage, and no drops, as yet, could penetrate to the earth.

"See, my boy, we are safe from the rain; nothing can reach us here," she said, cheering his despondency. "I will heap piles of dry wood on the fire, and shelter you all night long."

She paused a moment for flashes of blue lightening began to play fiercely through the thick foliage overhead, revealing depths of darkness that was enough to terrify a brave man. No wonder the boy shrank and trembled as it flashed and quivered over him.

Malaeska saw how frightened he was, and piled dry wood recklessly on the fire, hoping that its steady blaze would reassure him.

They were encamped on a spur of the Highlands that shot in a precipice over the stream, and the light of Malaeska's fire gleamed far and wide, casting a golden track far down the Hudson.

Four men, who were urging a boat bravely against the storm, saw the light, and shouted eagerly to each other.

"Here she is; nothing but an Indian would keep up a fire like that. Pull steadily and we have them."

They did pull steadily, and defying the storm, the boat made harbor under the cliff where Malaeska's fire still burned. Four men stole away from the boat, and crept stealthily up the hill, guided by the lightning and the gleaming fire above. The rain, beating among the branches, drowned their footsteps; and they spoke only in whispers, which were lost on the wind.

William had dropped asleep with tears on his thick eyelashes, which the strong firelight revealed to Malaeska, who regarded him with mournful affection. The cold wind chilled her through and through, but she did not feel it. So long as the boy slept comfortably she had no want.

I have said that the storm muffled all other sounds; and the four men who had left their boat at the foot of the cliff stood close by Malaeska before she had the least idea of their approach. Then a blacker shadow than fell from the pine, darkened the space around her,

36

and looking suddenly up, she saw the stern face of old Mr. Danforth between her and the firelight.

Malaeska did not speak or cry aloud, but snatching the sleeping boy close to her heart, lifted her pale face to his, half-defiant, half-terrified.

"Take my grandson from the woman and bring him down to the boat," said the old man, addressing those that came with him.

"No, no, he is mine!" cried Malaeska fiercely. "Nothing but the Great Spirit shall take him from me again!"

The sharp anguish in her voice awoke the boy. He struggled in her arms, and looking around, saw the old man.

"Grandfather, oh! grandfather take me home. I do want to go home," he cried stretching out his arms.

"Oh!" I have not the power of words to express the bitter anguish of that single exclamation, when it broke from the mother's pale lips. It was the cry of a heart that snapped its strongest fiber there and then. The boy wished to leave her. She had no strength after that, but allowed them to force him from her arms without a struggle. The rattlesnake had not paralyzed her so completely.

So they took the boy ruthlessly from her embrace, and carried him away. She followed after without a word of protest, and saw them lift him into the boat and push off, leaving her to the pitiless night. It was a cruel thing—bitterly cruel—but the poor woman was stupefied with the blow, and watched the boat with heavy eyes. All at once she heard the boy calling after her:

"Malaeska, come too. Malaeska—Malaeska!"

She heard the cry, and her icy heart swelled passionately With the leap of a panther she sprang to her own boat, and dashed after her tormenters, pulling fiercely through the storm. But with all her desperate energy, she was not able to overtake those four powerful men. They were out of sight directly, and she drifted after them alone—all alone.

Malaeska never went back to Mr. Danforth's house again, but she built a lodge on the Weehawken shore and supported herself by selling painted baskets and such embroideries as the Indians excel in. It was a lonely life, but sometimes she met her son in the streets of Manhattan, or sailing on the river, and this kept her alive.

After a few months, the lad came to her lodge. His grandmother consented to the visit, for she still had compassion on the lone Indian, and would not let the youth go beyond sea without bidding her farewell. In all the bitter anguish of that parting Malaeska kept her faith, and smothering the great want of her soul, saw her son depart without putting forth the holy claim of her motherhood. One day Malaeska stood upon the shore and saw a white-sailed ship veer from her moorings and pass away with cruel swiftness toward the ocean, the broad, boundless ocean, that seemed to her like eternity.

CHAPTER VII.

Alone in the forest, alone, When the night is dark and late— Alone on the waters, alone, She drifts to her woman's fate.

Again Malaeska took to her boat and, all alone, began her mournful journey to the forest. After the fight at Catskill, her brethren had retreated into the interior. The great tribe, which gave its name to the richest intervale in New York State, was always munificent in its hospitality to less fortunate brethren, to whom its hunting-grounds were ever open. Malaeska knew that her people were mustered somewhere near the amber-colored falls of Genesee, and she began her mournful voyage with vague longings to see them again, now that she had nothing but memories to live upon.

With a blanket in the bow of her boat, a few loaves of bread, and some meal in a coarse linen bag, she started up the river. The boat was battered and beginning to look old—half the gorgeous paint was worn from its sides, and the interior had been often washed by the tempest that beat over the little cove near her lodge where she had kept it moored. She made no attempt to remedy its desolate look. The tiger-skin was left behind in her lodge. No crimson cushions rendered the single seat tempting to sit upon. These fanciful comforts were intended for the boy—motherly love alone provided them; but now she had no care for things of this kind. A poor lone Indian woman, trampled on by the whites, deserted by her own child, was going back to her kinsfolk for shelter. Why should she attempt to appear less desolate than she was?

Thus, dreary and abandoned, Malaeska sat in her boat, heavily urging it up the stream. She had few wants, but pulled at the oars all day long, keeping time to the slow movement with her voice, from which a low funereal chant swelled continually.

Sometimes she went ashore, and building a fire in the loneliness, cooked the fish she had speared or the bird her arrow had brought down; but these meals always reminded her of the few happy days spent, after the sylvan fashion, with her boy, and she would sit moaning over the untasted food till the very birds that hovered near would pause in their singing to look askance at her. So she relaxed in her monotonous toil but seldom, and generally slept in her little craft, with the current rippling around her, and wrapped only in a coarse, gray blanket.

No one cared about her movements, and no one attempted to bring her back, or she might have been traced at intervals by some rock close to the shore, blackened with embers, where she had baked her corn-bread, or by the feathers of a bird which she had dressed, without caring to eat it.

Day after day—day after day, Malaeska kept on her watery path till she came to the mouth of the Mohawk. There she rested a little, with a weary, heavy-hearted dread of pursuing her journey further. What if her people should reject her as a renegade? She had deserted them in their hour of deep trouble—fled from the grave of her father, their chief, and had carried his grandson away to his bitterest enemy, the white man.

Would the people of her tribe forgive this treason, and take her back? She scarcely cared; life had become so dreary, the whole world so dark, that the poor soul rather courted pain, and would have smiled to know that death was near. Some vague ideas of religion, that the gentle grandmother of her son had taken pains to instill into that wild nature, kept her from self destruction; but she counted the probabilities that the tribe might put her to death, with vague hope.

Weary days, and more weary nights, she spent upon the Mohawk, creeping along the shadows and seeking the gloomiest spots for her repose: under the wild grape-vines that bent down the young elms with their purple fruit—under the golden willows and dusky pines she sought rest, never caring for danger; for, what had she to care how death or pain presented itself, so long as she had no fear of either?

At last she drew up her boat under a shelving precipice, and making it safe, took to the wilderness with nothing but a little corn meal, her blanket, and bow. With the same heavy listlessness that had marked her entire progress, she threaded the forest-paths, knowing by the hacked trees that her tribe had passed that way. But her path was rough, and the encampment far off, and she had many a heavy mile to walk before it could be reached. Her moccasins were worn to tatters, and her dress, once so gorgeous, all rent and weather

38

stained when she came in sight of the little prairie, hedged in by lordly forest-trees, in which her broken tribe had built their lodges.

Malaeska threw away her scant burden of food, and took a prouder bearing when she came in sight of those familiar lodges. In all her sorrow, she could not forget that she was the daughter of a great chief and a princess among the people which she sought.

Thus, with an imperial tread, and eyes bright as the stars, she entered the encampment and sought the lodge which, by familiar signs, she knew to be that of the chief who had superseded her son.

It was near sunset, and many of the Indian women had gathered in front of this lodge, waiting for their lords to come forth; for there was a council within the lodge, and like the rest of their sex, the dusky sisterhood liked to be in the way of intelligence. Malaeska had changed greatly during the years that she had been absent among the whites. If the lightness and grace of youth were gone, a more imposing dignity came in their place. Habits of refinement had kept her complexion clear and her hair bright. She had left them a slender, spirited young creature; she returned a serious woman, modest, but queenly withal.

The women regarded her first with surprise and then with kindling anger, for, after pausing to look at them without finding a familiar face, she walked on toward the lodge, and lifting the mat, stood within the opening in full view both of the warriors assembled there and the wrathful glances of the females on the outside.

When the Indians saw the entrance to their council darkened by a woman, dead silence fell upon them, followed by a fierce murmur that would have made a person who feared death tremble. Malaeska stood undismayed, surveying the savage group with a calm, regretful look; for among the old men, she saw some that had been upon the war-path with her father. Turning to one of these warriors, she said:

"It is Malaeska, daughter of the Black Eagle."

A murmur of angry surprise ran through the lodge and the women crowded together, menacing her with their glances.

"When my husband, the young white chief, died," continued Malaeska, "he told me to go down the great water and carry my son to his own people. The Indian wife obeys her chief."

A warrior, whom Malaeska knew as the friend of her father, arose with austere gravity, and spoke:

"It is many years since Malaeska took the young chief to his white fathers. The hemlock that was green has died at the top since then. Why does Malaeska come back to her people alone? Is the boy dead?"

Malaeska turned pale in the twilight, and her voice faltered. "The boy is not dead—yet Malaeska is alone!" she answered plaintively.

"Has the woman made a white chief of the boy? Has he become the enemy of our people?" said another of the Indians looking steadily at Malaeska.

Malaeska knew the voice and the look; it was that of a brave who, in his youth, had besought her to share his wigwam. A gleam of proud reproach came over her features, as she bent her head without answering.

Then the old chief spoke again. "Why does Malaeska come back to her tribe like a bird with its wings broken? Has the white chief driven her from his wigwam?"

Malaeska's voice broke out; the gentle pride of her character rose as the truth of her position presented itself.

"Malaeska obeyed the young chief, her husband, but her heart turned back to her own people. She tried to bring the boy into the forest again, but they followed her up the great river and took him away; Malaeska stands here alone."

Again the Indian spoke. "The daughter of the Black Eagle forsook her tribe when the death-song of her father was loud in the woods. She comes back when the corn is ripe, but there is no wigwam open to her. When a woman of the tribe goes off to the enemy, she returns only to die. Have I said well?"

A guttural murmur of assent ran through the lodge. The women heard it from their place in the open air, and gathering fiercely around the door, cried out, "Give her to us! She has stolen our chief—she has disgraced her tribe. It is long since we have danced at the fire-festival."

The rabble of angry women came on with their taunts and menaces, attempting to seize Malaeska, who stood pale and still before them; but the chief, whom she had once rejected, stood up, and with a motion of his hand repulsed them.

"Let the women go back to their wigwams. The daughter of a great chief dies only by the hands of a chief. To the warrior of her tribe, whom she has wronged, her life belongs."

Malaeska lifted her sorrowful eyes to his face—how changed it was since the day he had asked her to share his lodge.

"And it is you that want my life?" she said.

"By the laws of the tribe it is mine," he answered. "Turn your face to the east—it is growing dark; the forest is deep; no one shall hear Malaeska's cries when the hatchet cleaves her forehead. Come!"

Malaeska turned in pale terror, and followed him. No one interfered with the chief, whom she had refused for a white man. Her life belonged to him. He had a right to choose the time and place of her execution. But the women expressed their disappointment in fiendish sneers, as she glided like a ghost through their ranks and disappeared in the blackness of the forest.

Not a word was spoken between her and the chief. Stern and silent he struck into a trail which she knew led to the river, for she had travelled over it the day before. Thus, in darkness and profound silence, she walked on all night till her limbs were so weary that she longed to call out and pray the chief to kill her then and there; but he kept on a little in advance, only turning now and then to be sure that she followed.

Once she ventured to ask him why he put off her death so long; but he pointed along the trail, and walked along without deigning a reply. During the day he took a handful of parched corn from his pouch and told her to eat; but for himself, through that long night and day, he never tasted a morsel.

Toward sunset they came out on the banks of the Mohawk, near the very spot where she had left her boat. The Indian paused here and looked steadily at his victim.

The blood grew cold in Malaeska's veins—death was terrible when it came so near. She cast one look of pathetic pleading on his face, then, folding her hands, stood before him waiting for the moment.

"Malaeska!"

His voice was softened, his lips quivered as the name once so sweet to his heart passed through them.

"Malaeska, the river is broad and deep. The keel of your boat leaves no track. Go! the Great Spirit will light you with his stars. Here is corn and dried venison. Go in peace!"

She looked at him with her wild tender eyes; her lips began to tremble, her heart swelled with gentle sweetness, which was the grace of her civilization. She took the red hand of the savage and kissed it reverently.

"Farewell," she said; "Malaeska has no words; her heart is full."

The savage began to tremble; a glow of the old passion came over him.

"Malaeska, my wigwam is empty; will you go back? It is my right to save or kill."

Malaeska pointed upward to the sky.

"*He* is yonder, in the great hunting-ground, waiting for Malaeska to come. Could she go blushing from another chief's wigwam?"

For one instant those savage features were convulsed; then they settled down into the cold gravity of his former expression, and he pointed to the boat.

She went down to the edge of the water, while he took the blanket from his shoulders and placed it into the boat. Then he pushed the little craft from its mooring, and motioned her to jump in; he forbore to touch her hand, or even look on her face, but saw her take up the oars and leave the shore without a word; but when she was out of sight, his head fell forward on his bosom, and he gradually sank to an attitude of profound grief.

While he sat upon a fragment of rock, with a rich sunset crimsoning the water at his feet, a canoe came down the river, urged by a white man, the only one who over visited his tribe. This man was a missionary among the Indians, who held him in reverence as a great medicine chief, whose power of good was something to marvel at.

The chief beckoned to the missionary, who seemed in haste, but he drew near the shore. In a few brief but eloquent words the warrior spoke of Malaeska, of the terrible fate from which she had just been rescued, and of the forlorn life to which she must henceforth be consigned. There was something grand in this compassion that touched a thousand generous impulses in the missionary's heart. He was on his course down the river—for his duties lay with the Indians of many tribes—so he promised to overtake the lonely woman, to comfort and protect her from harm till she reached some settlement.

The good man kept his word. An hour after his canoe was attached to Malaeska's little craft by its slender cable, and he was conversing kindly with her of those things that interested his pure nature most.

Malaeska listened with meek and grateful attention. No flower ever opened to the sunshine more sweetly than her soul received the holy revelations of that good man. He had no time or place for teaching, but seized any opportunity that arose where a duty could be performed. His mission lay always where human souls required knowledge. So he never left the lonely woman till long after they had passed the mouth of the Mohawk, and were floating on the Hudson. When they came in sight of the Catskill range, Malaeska was seized with an irresistible longing to see the graves of her husband and father. What other place in the wide, wide world had she to look for? Where could she go, driven forth as she was by her own people, and by the father of her husband?

Surely among the inhabitants of the village she could sell such trifles as her inventive talent could create, and if any of the old lodges stood near "the Straka," that would be shelter enough.

With these thoughts in her mind, Malaeska took leave of the missionary with many a whispered blessing, and took her way to "the Straka." There she found an old lodge, through whose crevices the wind had whistled for years; but she went diligently to work, gathering moss and turf with which this old home, connected with so many sweet and bitter associations, was rendered habitable again. Then she took possession, and proceeded to invent many objects of comfort and even taste, with which to beautify the spot she had consecrated with memories of her passionate youth, and its early, only love.

The woods were full of game, and wild fruits were abundant; so that it was a long, long time before Malaeska's residence in the neighborhood was known. She shrank from approaching a people who had treated her so cruelly, and so kept in utter loneliness so long as solitude was possible.

In all her life Malaeska retained but one vague hope, and that was for the return of her son from that far-off country to which the cruel whites had sent him. She had questioned the missionary earnestly about these lands, and had now a settled idea of their extent and distance across the ocean. The great waters no longer seemed like eternity to her, or absence so much like death. Some time she might see her child again; till then she would wait and pray to the white man's God.

CHAPTER VIII.

Huzza for the forests and hills! Huzza, for the berries so blue! Our baskets we'll cheerily fill, While the thickets are sparkling with dew.

Years before the scene of our story returns to Catskill, Arthur Jones and the pretty Martha fellows had married and settled down in life. The kind-hearted old man died soon after the union, and left the pair inheritors of his little shop and of a respectable landed property. Arthur made an indulgent, good husband, and Martha soon became too much confined by the cares of a rising family, for any practice of the teasing coquetry which had characterized her girlhood. She seconded her husband in all his money-making projects; was an economical and thrifty housekeeper; never allowed her children to go barefooted, except in the very warmest weather; and, to use her own words, made a point of holding her head as high as any woman in the settlement.

If an uninterrupted course of prosperity could entitle a person to this privilege, Mrs. Jones certainly made no false claim to it. Every year added something to her husband's possessions. Several hundred acres of cleared land were purchased beside that which he inherited from his father-in-law; the humble shop gradually increased to a respectable variety-store, and a handsome frame-house occupied the site of the old log-cabin.

Besides all this, Mr. Jones was a justice of the peace and a dignitary in the village; and his wife, though a great deal stouter than when a girl, and the mother of six children, had lost none of her healthy good looks, and at the age of thirty-eight continued to be a very handsome woman indeed.

Thus was the family situated at the period when our story returns to them. One warm afternoon, in the depth of summer, Mrs. Jones was sitting in the porch of her dwelling occupied in mending a garment of home-made linen, which, from its size, evidently belonged to some one of her younger children. A cheese-press, with a rich heavy mass of curd compressed between the screws, occupied one side of the porch; and against it stood a small double flax-wheel, unbanded, and with a day's work yet unreeled from the spools. A hatchet and a pair of hand-cards, with a bunch of spools tied together by a tow string, lay in a corner, and high above, on rude wooden pegs, hung several enormous bunches of tow and linen yarn, the products of many weeks' hard labor.

Her children had gone into the woods after whortleberries, and the mother now and then laid down her work and stepped out to the green-sward beyond the porch to watch their coming, not anxiously, but as one who feels restless and lost without her usual

42

companions. After standing on the grass for awhile, shading her eyes with her hand and looking toward the woods, she at last returned to the porch, laid down her work, and entering the kitchen, filled the tea-kettle and began to make preparations for supper. She had drawn a long pine-table to the middle of the floor, and was proceeding to spread it, when her eldest daughter came through the porch, with a basket of whortleberries on her arm. Her pretty face was flushed with walking, and a profusion of fair tresses flowed in some disorder from her pink sun-bonnet, which was falling partly back from her head.

"Oh, mother, I have something so strange to tell you," she said, setting down the basket with its load of ripe, blue fruit, and fanning herself with a bunch of chestnut-leaves gathered from the woods. "You know the old wigwam by 'the Straka?' Well, when we went by it, the brush, which used to choke up the door, was all cleared off; the crevices were filled with green moss and leaves, and a cloud of smoke was curling beautifully up from the roof among the trees. We could not tell what to make of it, and were afraid to look in at first; but finally I peeped through an opening in the logs, and as true as you are here, mother, there sat an Indian woman reading—reading, mother! did you know that Indians could read? The inside of the wigwam was hung with straw matting, and there was a chest in it, and some stools, and a little shelf of books, and another with some earthen dishes and a china cup and saucer, sprinkled with gold, standing upon it. I did not see any bed, but there was a pile of fresh, sweet fern in one corner, with a pair of clean sheets spread on it, which I suppose she sleeps on, and there certainly was a feather pillow lying at the top.

"Well, the Indian woman looked kind and harmless; so I made an excuse to go in, and ask for a cup to drink out of.

"As I went round to the other side of the wigwam, I saw that the smoke came up from a fire on the outside; a kettle was hanging in the flame, and several other pots and kettles stood on a little bench by the trunk of an oak-tree, close by. I must have made some noise, for the Indian woman was looking toward the door when I opened it, as if she were a little afraid, but when she saw who it was, I never saw any one smile so pleasantly; she gave me the china cup, and went with me out to the spring where the boys were playing.

"As I was drinking, my sleeve fell back, and she saw the little wampum bracelet which you gave me, you know, mother. She started and took hold of my arm, and stared in my face, as if she would have looked me through; at last she sat down on the grass by the spring, and asked me to sit down by her and tell her my name. When I told her, she seemed ready to cry with joy; tears came into her eyes, and she kissed my hand two or three times, as if I had been the best friend she ever had on earth.

"I told her that a poor Indian girl had given the bracelet to you, before you were married to my father. She asked a great many questions about it, and you.

"When I began to describe the Indian fight, and the chief's grave down by the lake, she sat perfectly still till I had done; then I looked in her face; great tears were rolling one by one down her cheeks, her hands were locked in her lap, and her eyes were fixed upon my face with a strange stare, as if she did not know what she was gazing so hard at. She looked in my face, in this way, more than a minute after I had done speaking.

"The boys stopped their play, for they had begun to dam up the spring, and stood with their hands full of turf, huddled together, and staring at the poor woman as if they had never seen a person cry before. She did not seem to mind them, but went into the wigwam again without speaking a word."

"And was that the last you saw of her?" inquired Mrs. Jones who had become interested in her daughter's narration.

"Oh, no; she came out again just as we were going away from the spring. Her voice was more sweet and mournful than it had been, and her eyes looked heavy and troubled.

43

She thanked me for the story I had told her, and gave me this pair of beautiful moccasins."

"Mrs. Jones took the moccasins from her daughter's hand. They were of neatly dressed deer-skin, covered with beads and delicate needlework in silk.

"It is strange!" muttered Mrs. Jones; "one might almost think it possible. But nonsense; did not the old merchant send us word that the poor creature and her child were lost in the Highlands—that they died of hunger? Well, Sarah," she added, turning to her daughter, "is this all? What did the woman say when she gave you the moccasins? I don't wonder that you are pleased with them."

"She only told me to come again, and—"

Here Sarah was interrupted by a troop of noisy boys, who came in a body through the porch, flourishing their straw hats and swinging their whortleberry baskets, heavy with fruit, back and forth at each step.

"Hurra! hurra! Sarah's fallen in love with an old squaw. How do you do, Miss Jones? Oh, mother, I wish you could a seen her hugging and kissing the copper-skin—it was beautiful!"

Here the boisterous rogues set up a laugh that rang through the house, like the breaking up of a military muster.

"Mother, do make them be still; they have done nothing but tease and make fun of me all the way home," said the annoyed girl, half crying.

"How did the old squaw's lips taste, hey?" persisted the eldest boy, pulling his sister's sleeve, and looking with eyes full of saucy mischief up into her face. "Sweet as maple sugar wasn't it? Come, tell."

"Arthur—Arthur! you had better be quiet, if you know when you're well off!" exclaimed the mother, with a slight motion of the hand, which had a great deal of significant meaning to the mischievous group.

"Oh, don't—please, don't!" exclaimed the spoiled urchin, clapping his hands to his ears and running off to a corner, where he stood laughing in his mother's face. "I say Sarah, was it sweet?"

"Arthur, don't let me speak to you again, I say," cried Mrs. Jones, making a step forward and doing her utmost to get up a frown, while her hand gave additional demonstration of its hostile intent.

"Well, then, make her tell me; you ought to cuff her ears for not answering a civil question—hadn't she, boys!"

There was something altogether too ludicrous in this impudent appeal, and in the look of demure mischief put on by the culprit. Mrs. Jones bit her lips and turned away, leaving the boy as usual, victor of the field. "He isn't worth minding, Sarah," she said, evidently ashamed of her want of resolution; "come into the 'out-room,' I've something to tell you."

When the mother and daughter were alone, Mrs. Jones sat down and drew the young girl into her lap.

"Well, Sarah," she said, smoothing down the rich hair that lay against her bosom, "Your father and I have been talking about you to-day. You are almost sixteen, and can spin your day's work with any girl in the settlement. Your father says that after you have learned to weave and make cheese, he will send you down to Manhattan to school."

"Oh, mother, did he say so? in real, real, earnest?" cried the delighted girl flinging her arms round her mother's neck and kissing her yet handsome mouth with joy at the information it had just conveyed. "When will you let me go? I can learn to weave and make cheese in a week."

"If you learn all that he thinks best for you to know in two years, it will be as much as we expect. Eighteen is quite young enough. If you are very smart at home, you shall go when you are eighteen."

"Two years is a long, long time," said the girl, in a tone of disappointment; "but then father is kind to let me go at all. I will run down to the store and thank him. But, mother," she added, turning back from the door, "was there really any harm in talking with the Indian woman? There was nothing about her that did not seem like the whites but her skin, and that was not so *very* dark."

"Harm? No, child; how silly you are to let the boys tease you so."

"I will go and see her again, then—may I?"

"Certainly—but see; your father is coming to supper; run out and cut the bread. You must be very smart, now; remember the school."

During the time which intervened between Sarah Jones' sixteenth and eighteenth year, she was almost a daily visitor at the wigwam. The little footpath which led from the village to "the Straka," though scarcely definable to others, became as familiar to her as the grounds about her father's house. If a day or two passed in which illness or some other cause prevented her usual visit, she was sure to receive some token of remembrance from the lone Indian woman. Now, it reached her in the form of a basket of ripe fruit, or a bunch of wild flowers, tied together with the taste of an artist; again, it was a cluster of grapes, with the purple bloom lying fresh upon them, or a young mocking-bird, with notes as sweet as the voice of a fountain, would reach her by the hands of some village boy.

These affectionate gifts could always be traced to the inhabitant of the wigwam, even though she did not, as was sometimes the case, present them in person.

There was something strange in the appearance of this Indian woman, which at first excited the wonder, and at length secured the respect of the settlers. Her language was pure and elegant, sometimes even poetical beyond their comprehension, and her sentiments were correct in principle, and full of simplicity. When she appeared in the village with moccasins or pretty painted baskets for sale, her manner was apprehensive and timid as that of a child. She never sat down, and seldom entered any dwelling, preferring to sell her merchandise in the open air, and using as few words as possible in the transaction. She was never seen to be angry, and a sweet patient smile always hovered about her lips when she spoke. In her face there was more than the remains of beauty; the poetry of intellect and of warm, deep feeling, shed a loveliness over it seldom witnessed on the brow of a savage. In truth, Malaeska was a strange and incomprehensible being to the settlers. But she was so quiet, so timid and gentle, that they all loved her, bought her little wares, and supplied her wants as if she had been one of themselves.

There was something beautiful in the companionship which sprang up between the strange woman and Sarah Jones. The young girl was benefited by it in a manner which was little to be expected from an intercourse so singular and, seemingly, so unnatural. The mother was a kind-hearted worldly woman, strongly attached to her family, but utterly devoid of those fine susceptibilities which make at once the happiness and the misery of so many human beings. But all the elements of an intellectual, delicate, and high-souled woman slumbered in the bosom of her child. They beamed in the depths of her large blue eyes, broke over her pure white forehead, like perfume from the leaves of a lily, and made her small mouth eloquent with smiles and the beauty of unpolished thoughts.

45

At sixteen the character of the young girl had scarcely begun to develop itself; but when the time arrived when she was to be sent away to school, there remained little except mere accomplishments for her to learn. Her mind had become vigorous by a constant intercourse with the beautiful things of nature. All the latent properties of a warm, youthful heart, and of a superior intellect, had been gently called into action by the strange being who had gained such an ascendency over her feelings.

The Indian woman, who in herself combined all that was strong, picturesque, and imaginative in savage life, with the delicacy, sweetness, and refinement which follows in the train of civilization, had trod with her the wild-beautiful scenery of the neighborhood. They had breathed the pure air of the mountain together, and watched the crimson and amber clouds of sunset melt into evening, when pure sweet thoughts came to their hearts naturally, as light shines from the bosom of the star.

It is strange that the pure and simple religion which lifts the soul up to God, should have been first taught to the beautiful young white from the lips of a savage, when inspired by the dying glory of a sunset sky. Yet so it was; she had sat under preaching all her life, had imbibed creeds and shackled her spirit down with the opinions and traditions of other minds, nor dreamed that the love of God may sometimes kindle in the human heart, like fire flashing up from an altar-stone; and again, may expand gradually to the influence of the Divine Spirit, unfolding so gently that the soul itself scarcely knows at what time it burst into flower—that every effort we make, for the culture of the heart and the expanding of the intellect, is a step toward the attainment of religion if nothing more.

When the pure, simple faith of the Indian was revealed—when she saw how beautifully high energies and lofty feelings were mingled with the Christian meekness and enduring faith of her character, she began to love goodness for its own exceeding beauty, and to cultivate those qualities that struck her as so worthy in her wild-wood friend. Thus Sarah attained a refinement of the soul which no school could have given her, and no superficial gloss could ever conceal or dim. This refinement of principle and feeling lifted the young girl far out of her former commonplace associations; and the gentle influence of her character was felt not only in her father's household, but through all the neighborhood.

CHAPTER IX.

"She long'd for her mother's loving kiss, And her father's tender words, And her little sister's joyous mirth, Like the song of summer birds. Her heart went back to the olden home That her memory knew so well Till the veriest trifle of the past Swept o'er her like a spell."

Sarah Jones went to Manhattan at the appointed time, with a small trunk of clothing and a large basket of provisions; for a sloop in those days was a long time in coming down the Hudson, even with a fair wind, and its approach to a settlement made more commotion than the largest Atlantic steamer could produce at the present day. So the good mother provided her pretty pilgrim with a lading of wonder-cakes, with biscuits, dried beef, and cheese, enough to keep a company of soldiers in full ration for days.

Besides all this plenteousness in the commissary department, the good lady brought out wonderful specimens of her own handiwork in the form of knit muffles, fine yarn stockings, and colored wristlets, that she had been years in knitting for Sarah's outfit when she should be called upon to undertake this perilous adventure into the great world.

Beyond all this, Sarah had keepsakes from the children, with a store of pretty bracelets and fancy baskets from Malaeska, who parted with her in tenderness and sorrow; for one more like a wild grape-vine, putting out its tendrils everywhere for support, she was cast to the earth again.

After all, Sarah did not find the excitement of her journey so very interesting, and but for the presence of her father on the sloop, she would have been fairly homesick before the white sails of the sloop had rounded the Point. As it was, she grew thoughtful and almost sad as the somber magnificence of the scenery unrolled itself. A settlement here and there broke the forest with smiles of civilization, which she passed with proud consciousness of seeing the world; but, altogether, she thought more of the rosy mother and riotous children at home than of new scenes or new people.

At last Manhattan, with its girdle of silver waters, its gables and its overhanging trees, met her eager look. Here was her destiny—here she was to be taught and polished into a marvel of gentility. The town was very beautiful, but after the first novelty gave way, she grew more lonely than ever; every thing was so strange—the winding streets, the gay stores, and the quaint houses, with their peaks and dormer windows, all seeming to her far too grand for comfort.

To one of these houses Arthur Jones conducted his daughter, followed by a porter who carried her trunk on one shoulder, while Jones took charge of the provision-basket, in person.

There was nothing in all this very wonderful, but people turned to look at the group with more than usual interest, as it passed, for Sarah had all her mother's fresh beauty, with nameless graces of refinement, which made her a very lovely young creature to look upon.

When so many buildings have been raised in a city, so many trees uprooted, and ponds filled up, it is impossible to give the localities that formerly existed; for all the rural land-marks are swept away. But, in the olden times, houses had breathing space for flowers around them in Manhattan, and a man of note gave his name to the house he resided in. The aristocratic portion of the town was around the Bowling Green and back into the neighboring streets.

Somewhere in one of these streets, I can not tell the exact spot, for a little lake in the neighborhood disappeared soon after our story, and all the pretty points of the scene were destroyed with it—but somewhere, in one of the most respectable streets, stood a house with the number of gables and windows requisite to perfect gentility, and a large brass plate spread its glittering surface below the great brass knocker. This plate set forth, in bright, gold letters, the fact that Madame Monot, relict of Monsieur Monot who had so distinguished himself as leading teacher in one of the first female seminaries in Paris, could be found within, at the head of a select school for young ladies.

Sarah was overpowered by the breadth and brightness of this door-plate, and startled by the heavy reverberations of the knocker. There was something too solemn and grand about the entrance for perfect tranquillity.

Mr. Jones looked back at her, as he dropped the knocker, with a sort of tender self-complacency, for he expected that she would be rather taken aback by the splendor to which he was bringing her; but Sarah only trembled and grew timid; she would have given the world to turn and run away any distance so that in the end she reached home.

The door opened, at least the upper half, and they were admitted into a hall paved with little Dutch tiles, spotlessly clean, through which they were led into a parlor barren and prim in all its appointments, but which was evidently the grand reception-room of the establishment. Nothing could have been more desolate than the room, save that it was redeemed by two narrow windows which overlooked the angle of the green inclosure in

47

which the house stood. This angle was separated by a low wall from what seemed a broad and spacious garden, well filled with fruit-trees and flowering shrubbery.

The spring was just putting forth its first buds, and Sarah forgot the chilliness within as she saw the branches of a young apple-tree, flushed with the first tender green, drooping over the wall. It reminded her pleasantly of the orchard at home.

The door opened, and, with a nervous start, Sarah arose with her father to receive the little Frenchwoman who came in with a fluttering courtesy, eager to do the honors of her establishment.

Madame Monot took Sarah out of her father's hands with a graceful dash that left no room for appeal. "She knew it all—exactly what the young lady required—what would best please her very respectable parents—there was no need of explanations—the young lady was fresh as a rose—very charming—in a few months they should see—that was all—Monsieur Jones need have no care about his child—Madame would undertake to finish her education very soon—music, of course—an instrument had just come from Europe on purpose for the school—then French, nothing easier—Madame could promise that the young lady should speak French beautifully in one—two—three—four months, without doubt—Monsieur Jones might retire very satisfied—his daughter should come back different—perfect, in fact."

With all this volubility, poor Jones was half talked, half courtesied out of the house, without having uttered a single last word of farewell, or held his daughter one moment against the honest heart that yearned to carry her off again, despite his great ambition to see her a lady.

Poor Sarah gazed after him till her eyes were blinded with unshed tears; then she arose with a heavy heart and followed Madame to the room which was henceforth to be her refuge from the most dreary routine of duties that ever a poor girl was condemned to. It was a comfort that the windows overlooked that beautiful garden. That night, at a long, narrow table, set out with what the unsuspecting girl at first considered the preliminaries of a meal, Sarah met the score of young ladies who were to be her schoolmates. Fortunately she had no appetite and did not mind the scant fare. Fifteen or twenty girls, some furtively, others boldly, turning their eyes upon her, was enough to frighten away the appetite of a less timid person.

Poor Sarah! of all the homesick school-girls that ever lived, she was the most lonely. Madame's patronizing kindness only sufficed to bring the tears into her eyes which she was struggling so bravely to keep back.

But Sarah was courageous as well as sensitive. She came to Manhattan to study; no matter if her heart ached, the brain must work; her father had made great sacrifices to give her six months at this expensive school; his money and kindness must not be thrown away.

Thus the brave girl reasoned, and, smothering the haunting wish for home, she took up her tasks with energy.

Meantime Jones returned home with a heavy heart and a new assortment of spring goods, that threw every female heart in Catskill into a flutter of excitement. Every hen's nest in the neighborhood was robbed before the eggs were cold, and its contents transported to the store. As for butter, there was an universal complaint of its scarcity on the home table, while Jones began to think seriously of falling a cent on the pound, it came in so abundantly.

CHAPTER X.

'Twas a dear, old fashion'd garden, Half sunshine and half shade, Where all day long the birds and breeze A pleasant music made; And hosts of bright and glowing flower Their perfume shed around, Till it was like a fairy haunt That knew no human sound.— Frank Lee Benedict.

It was a bright spring morning, the sky full of great fleecy clouds that chased each other over the clear blue, and a light wind stirring the trees until their opening buds sent forth a delicious fragrance, that was like a perfumed breath from the approaching summer.

Sarah Jones stood by the window of her little room, looking wistfully out into the neighboring garden, oppressed by a feeling of loneliness and home-sickness, which made her long to throw aside her books, relinquish her half acquired accomplishments, and fly back to her quiet country home.

It seemed to her that one romp with her brothers through the old orchard, pelting each other with the falling buds, would be worth all the French and music she could learn in a score of years. The beat of her mother's lathe in the old fashioned loom, would have been pleasanter music to her ear, than that of the pianoforte, which she had once thought so grand an affair; but since then she had spent so many weary hours over it, shed so many tears upon the cold white keys, which made her fingers ache worse than ever the spinning-wheel had done, that, like any other school-girl, she was almost inclined to regard the vaunted piano as an instrument of torture, invented expressly for her annoyance.

She was tired of thinking and acting by rule, and though Madame Monot was kind enough in her way, the discipline to which Sarah was forced to submit, was very irksome to the untrained country girl. She was tired of having regular hours for study—tired of walking out for a stated time in procession with the other girls—nobody daring to move with anything like naturalness or freedom— and very often she felt almost inclined to write home and ask them to send for her.

It was in a restive, unhappy mood, like the one we have been describing, that she stood that morning at the window, when she ought to have been hard at work over the pile of books which lay neglected upon her little table.

That pretty garden which she looked down upon, was a sore temptation to her; and had Madame Monot known how it distracted Sarah's attention, there is every reason to believe that she would have been removed in all haste to the opposite side of the house, where if she chose to idle at her casement, there would be nothing more entertaining than a hard brick wall to look at. Just then, the garden was more attractive than at any other season of the year. The spring sunshine had made the shorn turf like a green carpet, the trim flower-beds were already full of early blossoms, the row of apple-trees was one great mass of flowers, and the tall pear-tree in the corner was just beginning to lose its delicate white leaves, sprinkling them daintily over the grass, where they fluttered about like a host of tiny butterflies.

The old-fashioned stoop that opened from the side of the house into the garden was covered with a wild grape-vine, that clambered up to the pointed Dutch gables, hung down over the narrow windows, and twined and tangled itself about as freely and luxuriantly as it could have done in its native forest.

Sarah watched the gardener as he went soberly about his various duties, and she envied him the privilege of wandering at will among the gravelled walks, pausing under the trees and bending over the flower-beds.

Perhaps in these days, when nothing but scentless japonicas and rare foreign plants are considered endurable, that garden would be an ordinary affair enough, at which no well-trained boarding-school miss would condescend to look for an instant; but to Sarah Jones it was a perfect little paradise.

The lilac bushes nodded in the wind, shaking their purple and white plumes, like groups of soldiers on duty; great masses of snowballs stood up in the center of the beds; peonies, violets, lilies of the valley, tulips, syringas, and a host of other dear old-fashioned flowers, lined the walks; and, altogether, the garden was lovely enough to justify the poor girl's admiration. There she stood, quite forgetful of her duties; the clock in the hall struck its warning note—she did not even hear it; some one might at any moment enter and surprise her in the midst of her idleness and disobedience—she never once thought of it, so busily was she watching every thing in the garden.

The man finished his morning's work and went away, but Sarah did not move. A pair of robins had flown into the tall pear-tree, and were holding an animated conversation, interspersed with bursts and gushes of song. They flew from one tree to another, once hovering near the grape-vine, but returned to the pear-tree at last, sang, chirped, and danced about in frantic glee, and at last made it evident that they intended to build a nest in that very tree. Sarah could have clapped her hands with delight! It was just under her window—she could watch them constantly, study or no study. She worked herself into such a state of excitement at the thought, that Madame Monot would have been shocked out of her proprieties at seeing one of her pupils guilty of such folly.

The clock again struck—that time in such a sharp, reproving way, that it reached even Sarah's ear. She started, looked nervously round, and saw the heap of books upon the table.

"Oh, dear me," she sighed; "those tiresome lessons! I had forgotten all about them. Well, I will go to studying in a moment," she added, as if addressing her conscience or her fears. "Oh, that robin—how he does sing."

She forgot her books again, and just at that moment there was a new object of interest added to those which the garden already possessed.

The side door of the house opened, and an old gentleman stepped out upon the broad stoop, stood there for a few moments, evidently enjoying the morning air, then passed slowly down the steps into the garden supporting himself by his stout cane, and walking with considerable care and difficulty, like any feeble old man.

Sarah had often seen him before, and she knew very well who he was. He was the owner of the house that the simple girl so coveted, and his name was Danforth.

She had learned every thing about him, as a school-girl is sure to do concerning any person or thing that strikes her fancy. He was very wealthy indeed, and had no family except his wife, the tidiest, darling old lady, who often walked in the garden herself, and always touched the flowers, as she passed, as if they had been pet children.

The venerable old pair had a grandson, but he was away in Europe, so they lived in their pleasant mansion quite alone, with the exception of a few domestics, who looked nearly as aged and respectable as their master and mistress.

Sarah had speculated a great deal about her neighbors. She did so long to know them, to be free to run around in their garden, and sit in the pleasant rooms that overlooked it, glimpses of which she had often obtained through the open windows, when the housemaid was putting things to rights.

Sarah thought that she might possibly be a little afraid of the old gentleman, he looked so stern; but his wife she longed to kiss and make friends with at once; she looked so gentle and kind, that even a bird could not have been afraid of her.

Sarah watched Mr. Danforth walk slowly down the principal garden-path, and seat himself in a little arbor overrun by a trumpet honeysuckle, which was not yet in blossom, although there were faint traces of red among the green leaves, which gave promise of an ample store of blossoms before many weeks.

He sat there some time, apparently enjoying the sunshine that stole in through the leaves. At length Sarah saw him rise, move toward the entrance, pause an instant, totter, then fall heavily upon the ground.

She did not wait even to cry out—every energy of her free, strong nature was aroused. She flew out of her room down the stairs, fortunately encountering neither teachers nor pupils, and hurried out of the street-door.

The garden was separated from Madame Monot's narrow yard by a low stone wall, along the top of which ran a picket fence. Sarah saw a step-ladder that had been used by a servant in washing windows; she seized it, dragged it to the wall, and sprang lightly from thence into the garden.

It seemed to her that she would never reach the spot where the poor gentleman was lying, although, in truth, scarcely three minutes had elapsed between the time that she saw him fall and reached the place where he lay.

Sarah stooped over him, raised his head, and knew at once what was the matter—he had been seized with apoplexy. She had seen her grandfather die with it, and recognized the symptoms at once. It was useless to think of carrying him, so she loosened his neckcloth, lifted his head upon the arbor seat, and darted toward the house, calling with all her might the name by which she had many times heard the gardener address the black cook. "Eunice! Eunice!"

At her frantic summons, out from the kitchen rushed the old woman, followed by several of her satellites, all screaming at once to know what was the matter, and wild with astonishment at the sight of a stranger in the garden.

"Quick! quick!" cried Sarah. "Your master has been taken with a fit; come and carry him into the house. One of you run for a doctor."

"Oh, de laws! oh, dear! oh, dear!" resounded on every side; but Sarah directed them with so much energy that the women, aided by an old negro who had been roused by the disturbance, conveyed their master into the house, and laid him upon a bed in one of the lower rooms.

"Where is your mistress?" questioned Sarah.

"Oh, she's gwine out," sobbed the cook; "oh, my poor ole massar, my poor ole massar!"

"Have you sent for the doctor?"

"Yes, young miss, yes; he'll be here in a minit; bress yer pooty face."

Sarah busied herself over the insensible man, applying every remedy that she could remember of having seen her mother use when her grandfather was ill, and really did the very things that ought to have been done.

It was not long before the doctor arrived, bled his patient freely, praised Sarah's presence of mind, and very soon the old gentleman returned to consciousness.

Sarah heard one of the servants exclaim: "Oh, dar's missus! praise de Lord!"

A sudden feeling of shyness seized the girl, and she stole out of the room and went into the garden, determined to escape unseen. But before she reached the arbor she heard one of the servants calling after her.

"Young miss! young miss! Please to wait; ole missus wants to speak to you."

Sarah turned and walked toward the house, ready to burst into tears with timidity and excitement. But the lady whom she had so longed to know, came down the steps and moved toward her, holding out her hand. She was very pale, and shaking from head to foot; but she spoke with a certain calmness, which it was evident she would retain under the most trying circumstances.

"I can not thank you," she said; "if it had not been for you, I should never have seen my husband alive again."

Sarah began to sob, the old lady held out her arms, and the frightened girl actually fell into them. There they stood for a few moments, weeping in each other's embrace, and by those very tears establishing a closer intimacy than years of common intercourse would have done.

"How did you happen to see him fall?" asked the old lady.

"I was looking out of my window," replied Sarah, pointing to her open casement, "and when I saw it I ran over at once."

"You are a pupil of Madame Monot's, then?"

"Yes—and, oh my, I must go back! They will scold me dreadfully for being away so long."

"Do not be afraid," said Mrs. Danforth, keeping fast hold of her hand when she tried to break away. "I will make your excuses to Madame; come into the house. I can not let you go yet."

She led Sarah into the house, and seated her in an easy chair in the old-fashioned sitting-room.

"Wait here a few minutes, if you please, my dear. I must go to my husband."

She went away and left Sarah quite confused with the strangeness of the whole affair. Here she was, actually seated in the very apartment she had so desired to enter—the old lady she had so longed to know addressing her as if she had been a favorite child.

She peeped out of the window toward her late prison; every thing looked quiet there, as usual. She wondered what dreadful penance she would be made to undergo, and decided that even bread and water for two days would not be so great a hardship, when she had the incident of the morning to reflect upon.

She looked about the room with its quaint furniture, every thing so tidy and elegant, looking as if a speck of dust had never by any accident settled in the apartment, and thinking it the prettiest place she had seen in her life.

Then she began thinking about the poor sick man, and worked herself into a fever of anxiety to hear tidings concerning him. Just then a servant entered with a tray of refreshments, and set it on the table near her, saying:

"Please, miss, my missus says you must be hungry, 'cause it's your dinner-time."

"And how is your master?" Sarah asked.

"Bery comfortable now; missee'll be here in a minute. Now please to eat sumfin."

Sarah was by no means loth to comply with the invitation, for the old cook had piled the tray with all sorts of delicacies, that presented a pleasing contrast to the plain fare she had been accustomed to of late.

52

By the time she had finished her repast Mrs. Danforth returned, looking more composed and relieved.

"The doctor gives me a great deal of encouragement," she said; "my husband is able to speak; by to-morrow he will thank you better than I can."

"Oh, no," stammered Sarah; "I don't want any thanks, please. I didn't think—I—"

She fairly broke down, but Mrs. Danforth patted her hand and said kindly:

"I understand. But at least you must let me love you very much."

Sarah felt her heart flutter and her cheeks glow. The blush and smile on that young face were a more fitting answer than words could have given.

"I have sent an explanation of your absence to Madame Monot," continued Mrs. Danforth, "and she has given you permission to spend the day with me; so you need have no fear of being blamed."

The thought of a whole day's freedom was exceedingly pleasant to Sarah, particularly when it was to be spent in that old house, which had always appeared as interesting to her as a story. It required but a short time for Mrs. Danforth and her to become well acquainted, and the old lady was charmed with her loveliness, and natural, graceful manners.

She insisted upon accompanying Mrs. Danforth into the sickroom, and made herself so useful there, that the dear lady mentally wondered how she had ever got on without her.

When Sarah returned to her home that night, she felt that sense of relief which any one who has led a monotonous life for months must have experienced, when some sudden event has changed its whole current, and given a new coloring to things that before appeared tame and insignificant.

During the following days Sarah was a frequent visitor at Mr. Danforth's house, and after that, circumstances occurred which drew her into still more intimate companionship with her new friend.

One of Madame Monot's house-servants was taken ill with typhus fever, and most of the young ladies left the school for a few weeks. Mrs. Danforth insisted upon Sarah's making her home at their house during the interval, an invitation which she accepted with the utmost delight.

Mr. Danforth still lingered—could speak and move—but the favorable symptoms which at first presented themselves had entirely disappeared, and there was little hope given that he could do more than linger for a month or two longer. During that painful season Mrs. Danforth found in Sarah a sympathizing and consoling friend, The sick man himself became greatly attached to her, and could not bear that she should even leave his chamber.

The young girl was very happy in feeling herself thus prized and loved, and the quick weeks spent in that old house were perhaps among the happiest of her life, in spite of the saddening associations which surrounded her.

One morning while she was sitting with the old gentleman, who had grown so gentle and dependent that those who had known him in former years would scarcely have recognized him, Mrs. Danforth entered the room, bearing several letters in her hand.

"European letters, my dear," she said to her husband, and while she put on her glasses and seated herself to read them, Sarah stole out into the garden.

She had not been there long, enjoying the fresh loveliness of the day, before she heard Mrs. Danforth call her.

"Sarah, my dear; Sarah."

The girl went back to the door where the old lady stood.

"Share a little good news with me in the midst of all our trouble," she said; "my dear boy—my grandson—is coming home."

Sarah's first thought was one of regret—every thing would be so changed by the arrival of a stranger; but that was only a passing pang of selfishness; her next reflection was one of unalloyed delight, for the sake of that aged couple.

"I am very glad, dear madame; his coming will do his grandfather so much good."

"Yes, indeed; more than all the doctors in the world."

"When do you expect him?"

"Any day, now; he was to sail a few days after the ship that brought these letters, and as this vessel has been detained by an accident, he can not be far away."

"I am to go back to school to-day," said Sarah, regretfully.

"But you will be with us almost as much," replied Mrs. Danforth. "I have your mother's permission, and will go myself to speak with Madame. You will run over every day to your lessons, but you will live here; we can not lose our pet so soon."

"You are very kind—oh, so kind," Sarah said, quite radiant at the thought of not being confined any longer in the dark old school-building.

"It is you who are good to us. But come, we will go over now; I must tell Madame Monot at once."

The explanations were duly made, and Sarah returned to her old routine of lessons; but her study-room was now the garden, or any place in Mr. Danforth's house that she fancied.

The old gentleman was better again; able to be wheeled out of doors into the sunshine; and there was nothing he liked so much as sitting in the garden, his wife knitting by his side, Sarah studying at his feet, and the robins singing in the pear-trees overhead, as if feeling it a sacred duty to pay their rent by morning advances of melody.

CHAPTER XI.

A welcome to the homestead— The gables and the trees; And welcome to the true hearts, As the sunshine and the breeze.

One bright morning, several weeks after Mr. Danforth's attack, the three were seated in their favorite nook in the garden.

It was a holiday with Sarah; there were no lessons to study; no exercises to practice; no duty more irksome than that of reading the newspaper aloud to the old gentleman, who particularly fancied her fresh, happy voice.

Mrs. Danforth was occupied with her knitting, and Sarah sat at their feet upon a low stool, looking so much like a favorite young relative that it was no wonder if the old pair forgot that she was unconnected with them save by the bonds of affection, and regarded her as being, in reality, as much a part of their family as they considered her in their hearts.

While they sat there, some sudden noise attracted Mrs. Danforth's attention; she rose and went into the house so quietly that the others scarcely noticed her departure.

It was not long before she came out again, walking very hastily for her, and with such a tremulous flutter in her manner, that Sarah regarded her in surprise.

"William!" she said to her husband, "William!"

He roused himself from the partial doze into which he had fallen, and looked up.

"Did you speak to me?" he asked.

"I have good news for you. Don't be agitated—it is all pleasant."

He struggled up from his seat, steadying his trembling hands upon his staff.

"My boy has come!" he exclaimed louder and more clearly than he had spoken for weeks; "William, my boy!"

At the summons, a young man came out of the house and ran toward them. The old gentleman flung his arms about his neck and strained him close to his heart.

"My boy!" was all he could say; "my William!"

When they had all grown somewhat calmer, Mrs. Danforth called Sarah, who was standing at a little distance.

"I want you to know and thank this young lady, William," she said; "your grandfather and I owe her a great deal."

She gave him a brief account of the old gentleman's fall, and Sarah's presence of mind; but the girl's crimson cheeks warned her to pause.

"No words can repay such kindness," said the young man, as he relinquished her hand, over which he had bowed with the ceremonious respect of the time.

"It is I who owe a great deal to your grandparents," Sarah replied, a little tremulously, but trying to shake off the timidity which she felt beneath his dark eyes. "I was a regular prisoner like any other school-girl, and they had the goodness to open the door and let me out."

"Then fidgety old Madame Monot had you in charge?" young Danforth said, laughing; "I can easily understand that it must be a relief to get occasionally where you are not obliged to wait and think by rule."

"There—there!" said the old lady; "William is encouraging insubordination already; you will be a bad counselor for Sarah."

Both she and her husband betrayed the utmost satisfaction at the frank and cordial conversation which went on between the young pair; and in an hour Sarah was as much at ease as if she had been gathering wild flowers in her native woods.

Danforth gave them long and amusing accounts of his adventures, talked naturally and well of the countries he had visited, the notable places he had seen, and never had man three more attentive auditors.

That was a delightful day to Sarah; and as William Danforth had not lost, in his foreign wanderings, the freshness and enthusiasm pleasant in youth, it was full of enjoyment to him likewise.

There was something so innocent in Sarah's loveliness—something so unstudied in her graceful manner, that the very contrast she presented to the artificial women of the world with whom he had been of late familiar, gave her an additional charm in the eye of the young man.

Many times, while they talked, Mrs. Danforth glanced anxiously toward her husband; but his smile reassured her, and there stole over her pale face a light from within which told of some pleasant vision that had brightened the winter season of her heart, and illuminated it with a reflected light almost as beautiful as that which had flooded it in its spring-time, when her dreams were of her own future, and the aged, decrepit man by her side a stalwart youth, noble and brave as the boy in whom their past seemed once more to live.

"If Madame Monot happens to see me she will be shocked," Sarah said, laughingly. "She told me that she hoped I would improve my holiday by reading some French sermons that she gave me."

"And have you looked at them?" Danforth asked.

"I am afraid they are mislaid," she replied, mischievously.

"Not greatly to your annoyance, I fancy? I think if I had been obliged to learn French from old-fashioned sermons, it would have taken me a long time to acquire the language."

"I don't think much of French sermons," remarked Mrs. Danforth, with a doubtful shake of the head.

"Nor of the people," added her husband; "you never did like them, Therese."

She nodded assent, and young Danforth addressed Sarah in Madame Monot's much-vaunted language. She answered him hesitatingly, and they held a little chat, he laughing good-naturedly at her mistakes and assisting her to correct them, a proceeding which the old couple enjoyed as much as the young pair, so that a vast amount of quiet amusement grew out of the affair.

They spent the whole morning in the garden, and when Sarah went up to her room for a time to be alone with the new world of thought which had opened upon her, she felt as if she had known William Danforth half her life. She did not attempt to analyze her feelings; but they were very pleasant and filled her soul with a delicious restlessness like gushes of agony struggling from the heart of a song-bird. Perhaps Danforth made no more attempt than she to understand the emotions which had been aroused within him; but they were both very happy, careless as the young are sure to be, and so they went on toward the beautiful dream that brightens every life, and which spread before them in the nearing future.

And so the months rolled on, and that pleasant old Dutch house grew more and more like a paradise each day. Another and another quarter was added to Sarah's school-term. She saw the fruit swell from its blossoms into form till its golden and mellow ripeness filled the garden with fragrance. Then she saw the leaves drop from the trees and take a thousand gorgeous dyes from the frost. Still the old garden was a paradise. She saw those leaves grow crisp and sere, rustling to her step with mournful sighs, and giving themselves with shudders to the cold wind. Still the garden was paradise. She saw the snow fall, white and cold, over lawn and gravel-walk, bending down the evergreens and tender shrubs, while long, bright icicles hung along the gables or broke into fragments on the ground beneath. Still the garden was paradise; for love has no season, and desolation is unknown where he exists, even though his sacred presence is unsuspected. Long before the promised period arrived, there was no falsehood in Madame Monot's assertion that her pupil should be perfect; for a lovelier or more graceful young creature than Sarah Jones could not well exist. How it would have been had she been entirely dependent on the school-teachers for her lessons, I can not pretend to say; but the pleasant studies which were so delicately aided in that old summer-house, while the old people sat by just out of ear-shot—as nice old people should on such occasions—were effective enough to build up half a dozen schools, if the progress of one pupil would suffice.

At such times old Mrs. Danforth would look up blandly from her work and remark in an innocent way to her husband, "That it was really beautiful to see how completely Sarah took to her lessons and how kindly William stayed at home to help her. Really," she thought, "traveling abroad did improve a person's disposition wonderfully. It gives a young man so much steadiness of character. There was William, now, who was so fond of excitement, and never could be persuaded to stay at home before, he could barely be driven across the threshold now."

The old man listened to these remarks with a keen look of the eye; he was asking himself the reason of this change in his grandson, and the answer brought a grim smile to his lips. The fair girl, who was now almost one of his household, had become so endeared to him that he could not bear the idea of even parting with her again, and the thought that the line of his name and property might yet persuade her to make the relationship closer still, had grown almost into a passion with the old man.

This state of things lasted only a few months. Before the leaves fell, a change came upon Mr. Danforth. He was for some time more listless and oppressed than usual, and seemed to be looking into the distance for some thought that had disturbed him. One day, without preliminaries, he began to talk with his wife about William's father, and, for the first time in years, mentioned his unhappy marriage.

"I have sometimes thought," said the lady, bending over her work to conceal the emotion that stirred her face, "I have sometimes thought that we should have told our grandson of all this years ago."

The old man's hand began to tremble on the top of his cane. His eyes grew troubled and he was a long time in answering.

"It is too late now—we must let the secret die with us. It would crush him forever. I was a proud man in those days," he said, at last; "proud and stubborn. God has smitten me therefore, I sometimes think. The thought of that poor woman, whose child I took away, troubles me at nights. Tell me Therese, if you know any thing about her. The day of my sickness I went to the lodge in Weehawken where she was last seen, hoping to find her, praying for time to make atonement; but the lodge was in ruins—no one could be found who even remembered her. It had cost me a great effort to go, and when the disappointment came, I fell beneath it. Tell me, Therese, if you have heard any thing of Malaeska?"

The good lady was silent; but she grew pale, and the work trembled in her hands.

"You will not speak?" said the old man, sharply.

"Yes," said the wife, gently laying down her work, and lifting her compassionate eyes to the keen face bending toward her, "I did hear, from some Indians that came to the fur-stations up the river, that an—that Malaeska went back to her tribe."

"There is something more," questioned the old man—"something you keep back."

The poor wife attempted to shake her head, but she could not, even by a motion, force herself to an untruth. So, dropping both hands in her lap, she shrunk away from his glance, and the tears began to roll down her cheeks.

"Speak!" said the old man, hoarsely.

She answered, in a voice low and hoarse as his own, "Malaeska went to her tribe; but they have cruel laws, and looking upon her as a traitor in giving her son to us, sent her into the woods with one who was chosen to kill her."

The old man did not speak, but his eyes opened wildly, and he fell forward upon his face.

William and Sarah were coquetting, with her lessons, under the old pear-tree, between the French phrases; he had been whispering something sweeter than words ever sounded to her before in any language, and her cheeks were one flush of roses as his breath floated over them.

"Tell me—look at me—any thing to say that you have known this all along," he said, bending his flashing eyes on her face with a glance that made her tremble.

57

She attempted to look up, but failed in the effort. Like a rose that feels the sunshine too warmly, she drooped under the glow of her own blushes.

"Do speak," he pleaded.

"Yes," she answered, lifting her face with modest firmness to his, "Yes, I do love you."

As the words left her lips, a cry made them both start.

"It is grandmother's voice; he is ill again," said the young man.

They moved away, shocked by a sudden recoil of feelings. A moment brought them in sight of the old man, who lay prostrate on the earth. His wife was bending over him, striving to loosen his dress with her withered little hands.

"Oh, come," she pleaded, with a look of helpless distress; "help me untie this, or he will never breathe again."

It was all useless; the old man never did breathe again. A single blow had smitten him down. They bore him into the house, but the leaden weight of his body, the limp fall of his limbs, all revealed the mournful truth too plainly. It was death—sudden and terrible death.

If there is an object on earth calculated to call forth the best sympathies of humanity, it is an "old widow"—a woman who has spent the spring, noon, and autumn of life, till it verges into winter, with one man, the first love of her youth, the last love of her age—the spring-time when love is a passionate sentiment, the winter-time when it is august.

In old age men or women seldom resist trouble—it comes, and they bow to it. So it was with this widow: she uttered no complaints, gave way to no wild outbreak of sorrow— "she was lonesome—very lonesome without him," that was all her moan; but the raven threads that lay in the snow of her hair, were lost in the general whiteness before the funeral was over, and after that she began to bend a little, using his staff to lean on. It was mournful to see how fondly her wrinkled hands would cling around the head, and the way she had of resting her delicate chin upon it, exactly as he had done.

But even his staff, the stout prop of his waning manhood, was not strong enough to keep that gentle old woman from the grave. She carried it to the last, but one day it stood unused by the bed, which was white and cold as the snow-drift through which they dug many feet before they could lay her by her husband's side.

CHAPTER XII.

Put blossoms on the mantle-piece, Throw sand upon the floor, A guest is coming to the house, That never came before.

Sarah Jones had been absent several months, when a rumor got abroad in the village, that the school-girl had made a proud conquest in Manhattan. It was said that Squire Jones had received letters from a wealthy merchant of that place, and that he was going down the river to conduct his daughter home, when a wedding would soon follow, and Sarah Jones be made a lady.

This report gained much of its probability from the demeanor of Mrs. Jones. Her port became more lofty when she appeared in the street, and she was continually throwing out insinuations and half-uttered hints, as if her heart were panting to unburden itself of some proud secret, which she was not yet at liberty to reveal.

When Jones actually started for Manhattan, and it was whispered about that his wife had taken a dress-pattern of rich chintz from the store, for herself, and had bought each of the boys a new wool hat, conjecture became almost certainty; and it was asserted boldly, that Sarah Jones was coming home to be married to a man as rich as all out-doors, and that her mother was beginning to hold her head above common folks on the strength of it.

About three weeks after this report was known, Mrs. Jones, whose motions were watched with true village scrutiny, gave demonstrations of a thorough house-cleaning. An old woman, who went out to days' work, was called in to help, and there were symptoms of slaughter observable in the barn-yard one night after the turkeys and chickens had gone to roost; all of which kept the public mind in a state of pleasant excitement. Early the next morning, after the barn-yard massacre, Mrs. Jones was certainly a very busy woman. All the morning was occupied in sprinkling white sand on the nicely-scoured floor of the out-room, or parlor, which she swept very expertly into a series of angular figures called herring-bones, with a new splint broom. After this, she filled the fire-place with branches of hemlock and white pine, wreathed a garland of asparagus, crimson with berries, around the little looking-glass, and, dropping on one knee, was filling a large pitcher on the hearth from an armful of wild-flowers, which the boys had brought her from the woods, when the youngest son came hurrying up from the Point, to inform her that a sloop had just hove in sight and was making full sail up the river.

"Oh, dear, I shan't be half ready!" exclaimed the alarmed housekeeper, snatching up a handful of meadow-lilies, mottled so heavily with dark-crimson spots, that the golden bells seemed drooping beneath a weight of rubies and small garnet stones, and crowding them down into the pitcher amid the rosy spray of wild honeysuckle-blossom, and branches of flowering dogwood.

"Here, Ned, give me the broom, quick! and don't shuffle over the sand so. There, now," she continued, gathering up the fragments of leaves and flowers from the hearth, and glancing hastily around the room, "I wonder if any thing else is wanting?"

Every thing seemed in order, even to her critical eye. The tea-table stood in one corner, its round top turned down and its polished surface reflecting the herring-bones drawn in the sand, with the distinctness of a mirror. The chairs were in their exact places, and the new crimson moreen cushions and valance decorated the settee, in all the brilliancy of their first gloss. Yes nothing more was to be done, still the good woman passed her apron over the speckless table and flirted it across a chair or two, before she went out, quite determined that no stray speck of dust should disgrace her child on coming home.

Mrs. Jones closed the door, and hurried up to the square bedroom, to be certain that all was right there also. A patchwork quilt, pieced in what old ladies call "a rising sun," radiated in tints of red, green, and yellow, from the center of the bed down to the snow-white valances. A portion of the spotless homespun sheet was carefully turned over the upper edge of the quilt, and the whole was surmounted by a pair of pillows, white as a pile of newly-drifted snow-flakes. A pot of roses, on the window-sill, shed a delicate reflection over the muslin curtains looped up on either side of the sash; and the fresh wind, as it swept through, scattered their fragrant breath deliciously through the little room.

Mrs. Jones gave a satisfied look and then hurried to the chamber prepared for her daughter, and began to array her comely person in the chintz dress, which had created such a sensation in the village. She had just encased her arms in the sleeves, when the door partly opened, and the old woman, who had been hired for a few days as "help," put her head through the opening. "I say, Miss Jones, I can't find nothin' to make the stuffin' out on."

"My goodness! isn't that turkey in the oven yet? I do believe, if I could be cut into a hundred pieces, it wouldn't be enough for this house. What do you come to me for?—don't you know enough to make a little stuffing without my help?"

"Only give me enough to do it with, and if I don't, why, there don't nobody, that's all; but I've been a looking all over for some sausengers, and can't find none, nowhere."

"Sausages? Why, Mrs. Bates, you don't think that I would allow that fine turkey to be stuffed with sausages?"

"I don't know nothin' about it, but I tell you just what it is, Miss Jones, if you are a-growing so mighty partic'lar about your victuals, just cause your darter's a-coming home with a rich beau, you'd better cook 'em yourself; nobody craves the job," retorted the old woman, in her shrillest voice, shutting the door with a jar that shook the whole apartment.

"Now the cross old thing will go off just to spite me," muttered Mrs. Jones, trying to smother her vexation, and, opening the door, she called to the angry "help:"

"Why, Mrs. Bates, do come back, you did not stay to hear me out. Save the chickens' liver and chop them up with bread and butter; season it nicely, and I dare say, you will be as well pleased with it as can be."

"Well, and if I du, what shall I season with—sage or summer-savory? I'm sure I'm willing to du my best," answered the partially mollified old woman.

"A little of both, Mrs. Bates—oh, dear! won't you come back and see if you can make my gown meet? There—do I look fit to be seen?"

"Now, what do you ask that for Miss Jones? you know you look as neat as a new pin. This is a mighty purty calerco, ain't it, though?"

The squire's lady had not forgotten all the feelings of her younger days. And the old woman's compliment had its effect.

"I will send down to the store for some tea and molasses for you to take home to-night, Mrs. Bates, and—"

"Mother! mother!" shouted young Ned, bolting into the room, "the sloop has tacked, and is making for the creek. I see three people on the deck, and I'm almost sure father was one of them—they will be here in no time."

"Gracious me!" muttered the old woman, hurrying away to the kitchen.

Mrs. Jones smoothed down the folds of her new dress with both hands, as she ran down to the "out-room." She took her station in a stiff, high-backed chair by the window, with a look of consequential gentility, as if she had done nothing but sit still and receive company all her life.

After a few minutes' anxious watching, she saw her husband and daughter coming up from the creek, accompanied by a slight, dark, and remarkably graceful young man, elaborately, but not gayly dressed, for the fashion of the time, and betraying even in his air and walk peculiar traits of high-breeding and refinement. His head was slightly bent, and he seemed to be addressing the young lady who leaned on his arm.

The mother's heart beat high with mingled pride and affection, as she gazed on her beautiful daughter thus proudly escorted home. There was triumph in the thought, that almost every person in the village might witness the air of gallantry and homage with which she was regarded by the handsomest and richest merchant of Manhattan. She saw that her child looked eagerly toward the house as they approached, and that her step was rapid, as if impatient of the quiet progress of her companions. Pride was lost in the sweet thrill of maternal affection which shot through the mother's heart. She forgot all her plans, in the dear wish to hold her first-born once more to her bosom; and ran to the door, her face beaming with joy, her arms outstretched, and her lips trembling with the warmth of their own welcome.

The next moment her child was clinging about her, lavishing kisses on her handsome mouth, and checking her caresses to gaze up through the mist of tears and smiles which deluged her own sweet face, to the glad eyes that looked down so fondly upon her.

"Oh, mother! dear, dear mother, how glad I am to get home! Where are the boys? where is little Ned?" inquired the happy girl, rising from her mother's arms, and looking eagerly round for other objects of affectionate regard.

"Sarah, don't you intend to let me speak to your mother?" inquired the father, in a voice which told how truly his heart was in the scene.

Sarah withdrew from her mother's arms, blushing and smiling through her tears; the husband and wife shook hands half a dozen times over; Mrs. Jones asked him how he had been, what kind of a voyage he had made, how he liked Manhattan, and a dozen other questions, all in a breath: and then the stranger was introduced. Mrs. Jones forgot the dignified courtesy which she had intended to perpetrate on the entrance of her guest, and shook him heartily by the hand, as if she had been acquainted with him from his cradle.

When the happy group entered the parlor, they found Arthur, who had been raised to the dignity of storekeeper in the father's absence, ready to greet his parent and sister; and the younger children huddled together at the door which led to the kitchen, brimful of joy at the father's return, and yet too much afraid of the stranger to enter the room.

Altogether, it was as cordial, warm-hearted a reception as a man could reasonably wish on his return home; and, fortunately for Mrs. Jones, the warmth of her own natural feeling saved her the ridicule of trying to get up a genteel scene, for the edification of her future son-in-law.

About half an hour after the arrival of her friends, Mrs. Jones was passing from the kitchen, where she had seen the turkey placed in the oven, with its portly bosom rising above the rim of a dripping-pan, his legs tied together, and his wings tucked snugly over his back, when she met her husband in the passage.

"Well," said the wife, in a cautious voice, "has every thing turned out well—is he so awful rich as your letter said?"

"There can be no doubt about that; he is as rich as a Jew, and is proud as a lord. I can tell you what, Sarah's made the best match in America, let the other be what it will," replied the squire, imitating the low tone of his questioner.

"What an eye he's got, hasn't he; I never saw any thing so black and piercing in my life. He's very handsome, too, only a little darkish—I don't wonder the girl took a fancy to him. I say, has any thing been said about the wedding?"

"It must be next week, for he wants to go back to Manhattan in a few days; he and Sarah will manage that without our help, I dare say." Here Mr. and Mrs. Jones looked at each other and smiled.

"I say, squire, I want to ask you one question," interrupted Mrs. Bates, coming through the kitchen door and sidling up to the couple, "is that watch which the gentleman carries rale genuine gold, or on'y pinchbeck? I'd give any thing on 'arth to find out."

"I believe it's gold, Mrs. Bates."

"Now, du tell! What, rale Guinea gold? Now, if that don't beat all natur. I ruther guess Miss Sarah's feathered her nest this time, any how. Now, squire, du tell a body, when is the wedding to be? I won't tell a single 'arthly critter, if you'll on'y jest give me a hint."

"You must ask Sarah," replied Mr. Jones, following his wife into the parlor; "I never meddle with young folks' affairs."

"Now, did you ever?" muttered the old woman, when she found herself alone in the passage. "Never mind; if I don't find out afore I go home to-night, I lose my guess, that's all. I should just like to know what they're a talking about this minute."

Here the old woman crouched down and put her ear to the crevices under the parlor door; in a few moments she scrambled up and hurried off into the kitchen again, just in time to save herself from being pushed over by the opening door.

Sarah Jones returned home the same warm-hearted, intelligent girl as ever. She was a little more delicate in person, more quiet and graceful in her movements; and love had given depth of expression to her large blue eyes, a richer tone to her sweet voice, and had mellowed down the buoyant spirit of the girl to the softness and grace of womanhood. Thoroughly and trustfully had she given her young affections, and her person seemed imbued with gentleness from the fount of love, that gushed up so purely in her heart. She knew that she was loved in return—not as she loved, fervently, and in silence, but with a fire of a passionate nature; with the keen, intense feeling which mingles pain even with happiness, and makes sorrow sharp as the tooth of a serpent.

Proud, fastidious, and passionate was the object of her regard; his prejudices had been strengthened and his faults matured, in the lap of luxury and indulgence. He was high spirited and generous to a fault, a true friend and a bitter enemy—one of those men who have lofty virtues and strong counterbalancing faults. But with all his heart and soul he loved the gentle girl to whom he was betrothed. In that he had been thoroughly unselfish and more than generous; but not the less proud. The prejudices of birth and station had been instilled into his nature, till they had become a part of it; yet he had unhesitatingly offered hand and fortune to the daughter of a plain country farmer.

In truth, his predominating pride might be seen in this, mingled with the powerful love which urged him to the proposal. He preferred bestowing wealth and station on the object of his choice, rather than receiving any worldly advantage from her. It gratified him that his love would be looked up to by its object, as the source from which all benefits must be derived. It was a feeling of refined selfishness; he would have been startled had any one told him so; and yet, a generous pride was at the bottom of all. He gloried in exalting his chosen one; while his affianced wife, and her family, were convinced that nothing could be more noble than his conduct, in thus selecting a humble and comparatively portionless girl to share his fortune.

On the afternoon of the second day after her return home, Sarah entered the parlor with her bonnet on and shawl flung over her arm, prepared for a walk. Her lover was lying on the crimson cushions of the settee, with his fine eyes half closed, and a book nearly falling from his listless hand.

"Come," said Sarah, taking the volume playfully from his hand, "I have come to persuade you to a long walk. Mother has introduced all her friends, now you must go and see mine—the dearest and best."

"Spare me," said the young man, half-rising, and brushing the raven hair from his forehead with a graceful motion of the hand; "I will go with *you* anywhere, but *do* excuse me these horrid introductions—I am overwhelmed with the hospitality of your neighborhood." He smiled, and attempted to regain the book as he spoke.

"Oh, but this is quite another kind of person; you never saw any thing at all like her—there is something picturesque and romantic about her. You like romance?"

"What is she, Dutch or English? I can't speak Dutch and your own sweet English is enough for me. Come, take off that bonnet and let me read to you."

"No no; *I* must visit the wigwam, if *you* will not."

"The wigwam, Miss Jones?" exclaimed the youth, starting up, his face changing its expression, and his large black eyes flashing on her with the glance of an eagle. "Am I to understand that your friend is an Indian?"

"Certainly, she *is* an Indian, but not a common one I assure you."

"She *is* an Indian. Enough, *I* will *not* go; and I can only express my surprise at a request so extraordinary. I have no ambition to cultivate the copper-colored race, or to find my future wife seeking her friends in the woods."

The finely cut lip of the speaker curved with a smile of haughty contempt, and his manner was disturbed and irritable, beyond anything the young girl had ever witnessed in him before. She turned pale at his violent burst of feeling, and it was more than a minute before she addressed him again.

"This seems violence unreasonable—why should my wish to visit a harmless, solitary fellow-being create so much opposition," she said, at last.

"Forgive me, if I have spoken harshly, dear Sarah," he answered, striving to subdue his irritation, but spite of his effort it blazed out again, the next instant. "It is useless to strive against the feeling; I hate the whole race! If there is a thing I abhor on earth, it is a savage—a fierce, blood-thirsty wild beast in human form!"

There was something in the stern expression of his face, which pained and startled the young girl who gazed on it; a brilliancy of the eye, and an expansion of the thin nostrils, which bespoke terrible passions when once excited to the full.

"This is a strange prejudice," she murmured, unconsciously, while her eyes sank from their gaze on his face.

"It is no prejudice, but a part of my nature," he retorted, sternly, pacing up and down the room. "An antipathy rooted in the cradle, which grew stronger and deeper with my manhood. I loved my grandfather, and from him I imbibed this early hate. His soul loathed the very name of Indian. When he met one of the prowling creatures in the highway, I have seen his lips writhe, his chest heave, and his face grow white, as if a wild beast had started up in his path. There was one in our family, an affectionate, timid creature, as the sun ever shone upon. I can remember loving her very dearly when I was a mere child, but my grandfather recoiled at the very sound of her name, and seemed to regard her presence as a curse, which for some reason he was compelled to endure. I could never imagine why he kept her. She was very kind to me, and I tried to find her out after my return from Europe, but you remember that my grandparents died suddenly during my absence, and no one could give me any information about her. Save that one being, there is not a savage, male or female, whom I should not rejoice to see exterminated from the face of the earth. Do not, I pray you, look so terribly shocked, my sweet girl; I acknowledge the feeling to be a prejudice too violent for adequate foundation, but it was grounded in my nature by one whom I respected and loved as my own life, and it will cling to my heart as long as there is a pulse left in it."

"I have no predeliction for savages as a race," said Sarah, after a few moments' silence, gratified to find some shadow of reason for her lover's violence; "but you make one exception, may I not also be allowed a favorite? especially as she is a white in education, feeling everything but color? You would not have me neglect one of the kindest, best friends I ever had on earth, because the tint of her skin is a shade darker than my own?"

Her voice was sweet and persuasive, a smile trembled on her lips, and she laid a hand gently on his arm as she spoke. He must have been a savage indeed, had he resisted her winning ways.

"I would have you forgive my violence and follow your own sweet impulses," he said, putting back the curls from her uplifted forehead, and drawing her to his bosom; "say you have forgiven me, dear, and then go where you will."

These words could hardly be called a lovers' quarrel, and yet they parted with all the sweet feelings of reconciliation, warm at the heart of each.

CHAPTER XIII.

By the forest-grave she mournful stood, While her soul went forth in prayer; Her life was one long solitude, Which she offer'd, meekly, there.

Sarah pursued the foot-path, which she had so often trod through the forest, with a heart that beat quicker at the sight of each familiar bush or forest-tree.

"Poor woman, she must have been very lonely," she murmured, more than once, when the golden blossoms of a spice-bush, or the tendrils of a vine trailing over the path, told how seldom it had been traveled of late, and her heart imperceptibly became saddened by the thoughts of her friend.

To her disappointment, she found the wigwam empty, but a path was beaten along the edge of the woods, leading toward the Pond, which she had never observed before. She turned into it with a sort of indefinite expectation of meeting her friend; and after winding through the depth of the forest for nearly a mile, the notes of a wild, plaintive song rose and fell—a sad, sweet melody—on the still air.

A few steps onward brought the young girl to a small open space surrounded by young saplings and flowering shrubs; tall grass swept from a little mound which swelled up from the center, to the margin of the inclosure, and a magnificent hemlock shadowed the whole space with its drooping boughs.

A sensation of awe fell upon the heart of the young girl, for, as she gazed, the mound took the form of a grave. A large rose-tree, heavy with blossoms, drooped over the head, and the sheen of rippling waters broke through a clump of sweet-brier, which hedged it in from the lake.

Sarah remembered that the Indian chief's grave was on the very brink of the water, and that she had given a young rose-tree to Malaeska years ago, which must have shot up into the solitary bush standing before her, lavishing fragrance from its pure white flowers over the place of the dead.

This would have been enough to convince her that she stood by the warrior's grave, had the place been solitary, but at the root of the hemlock, with her arms folded on her bosom and her calm face uplifted toward heaven, sat Malaeska. Her lips were slightly parted, and the song which Sarah had listened to afar off broke from them—a sad pleasant strain, that blended in harmony with the rippling waters and the gentle sway of the hemlock branches overhead.

Sarah remained motionless till the last note of the song died away on the lake, then she stepped forward into the inclosure. The Indian woman saw her and arose, while a beautiful expression of joy beamed over her face.

"The bird does not feel more joyful at the return of spring, when snows have covered the earth all winter, than does the poor Indian's heart at the sight of her child again," she said, taking the maiden's hand and kissing it with a graceful movement of mingled respect and affection. "Sit down, that I may hear the sound of your voice once more."

They sat down together at the foot of the hemlock.

"You have been lonely, my poor friend, and ill, I fear; how thin you have become during my absence," said Sarah, gazing on the changed features of her companion.

64

"I shall be happy again now," replied the Indian, with a faint sweet smile, "you will come to see me every day."

"Yes, while I remain at home, but—but—I'm going back again soon."

"You need not tell me more in words, I can read it in the tone of your voice, in the light of that modest eye,—in the color coming and going on those cheeks; another is coming to take you from home," said the Indian, with a playful smile. "Did you think the lone woman could not read the signs of love—that she has never loved herself?

"You?"

"Do not look so wild, but tell me of yourself. Are you to be married so *very* soon?"

"In four days."

"Then where will your home be?"

"In Manhattan."

There were a few moments of silence. Sarah sat gazing on the turf, with the warm blood mantling to her cheek, ashamed and yet eager to converse more fully on the subject which flooded her young heart with supreme content. The Indian continued motionless, lost in a train of sad thoughts conjured up by the last word uttered; at length she laid her hand on that of her companion, and spoke; her voice was sad, and tears stood in her eyes.

"In a few days you go from me again—oh, it is very wearisome to be always alone; the heart pines for something to love. I have been petting a little wren, that has built his nest under the eaves of my wigwam, since you went away; it was company for me, and will be again. Do not look so pitiful, but tell me who is he that calls the red blood to your cheek? Does he love you? Is he good, brave?"

"He says that he loves me," replied the young girl, blushing more deeply.

"And you?"

"If to think of one from morning to night, be love—to know that he is haunting your beautiful day-dreams, wandering with you through the lovely places which fancy is continually presenting to one in solitude, filling up each space and thought of your life, and yet in no way diminishing the affection which the heart bears to others, but increasing it rather—if to be made happy with the slightest trait of noble feeling, proud in his virtues, and yet quick-sighted and doubly sensitive to all his faults, clinging to him in spite of those faults—if this be love, then I do love with the whole strength of my being. My heart is full of tranquillity, and, like that white rose which lies motionless in the sunshine burdened with the wealth of its own sweetness, it unfolds itself day by day to a more pure and subdued state of enjoyment This feeling may not be the love which men talk so freely of, but it can not change—never—not even in death, unless William Danforth should prove utterly unworthy!"

"William Danforth! Did I hear you aright? Is William Danforth the name of your affianced husband?" inquired the Indian, in a voice of overwhelming surprise, starting up with sudden impetuosity and then slowly sinking back to her seat again. "Tell me," she added, faintly, and yet in a tone that thrilled to the heart, "has this boy—this young gentleman, I mean—come of late from across the big waters?"

"He came from Europe a year since, on the death of his grandparents," was the reply.

"A year, a whole year!" murmured the Indian, clasping her hands over her eyes with sudden energy. Her head sunk forward upon her knees, and her whole frame shivered with a rush of strong feeling, which was perfectly unaccountable to the almost terrified girl who gazed upon her. "Father of Heaven, I thank thee! my eyes shall behold him once more. O God, make me grateful!" These words, uttered so fervently, were muffled by the locked hands of the Indian woman, and Sarah could only distinguish that she was strongly excited by the mention of her lover's name.

"Have you ever known Mr. Danforth?" she inquired, when the agitation of the strange woman had a little subsided. The Indian did not answer, but raising her head, and brushing the tears from her eyes, she looked in the maiden's face with an expression of pathetic tenderness that touched her to the heart.

"And *you* are to be *his* wife? You, my bird of birds."

She fell upon the young girl's neck as she spoke, and wept like an infant; then, as if conscious of betraying too deep emotion, she lifted her head, and tried to compose herself; while Sarah sat gazing on her, agitated, bewildered, and utterly at a loss to account for this sudden outbreak of feeling, in one habitually so subdued and calm in her demeanor. After sitting musingly and in silence several moments, the Indian again lifted her eyes; they were full of sorrowful meaning, yet there was an eager look about them which showed a degree of excitement yet unsubdued.

"Dead—are they both dead? his grandparents, I mean?" she said, earnestly.

"Yes, they are both dead; he told me so."

"And he—the young man—where is he now?"

"I left him at my father's house, not three hours since."

"Come, let us go."

The two arose, passed through the inclosure, and threaded the path toward the wigwam slowly and in silence.

The afternoon shadows were gathering over the forest, and being anxious to reach home before dark, Sarah refused to enter the wigwam when they reached it. The Indian went in for a moment, and returned with a slip of birch bark, on which a few words were lightly traced in pencil.

"Give this to the young man," she said, placing the bark in Sarah's hand; "and now good-night—good-night."

Sarah took the bark and turned with a hurried step to the forest track. She felt agitated, and as if something painful were about to happen. With a curiosity aroused by the Indian's strange manner, she examined the writing on the slip of bark in her hand; it was only a request that William Danforth would meet the writer at a place appointed, on the bank of the Catskill Creek, that evening. The scroll was signed, "Malaeska."

Malaeska! It was singular, but Sarah Jones had never learned the Indian's name before.

CHAPTER XIV.

The point of land, which we have described in the early part of this story, as hedging in the outlet of Catskill Creek, gently ascends from the juncture of the two streams and rolls upward into a broad and beautiful hill, which again sweeps off toward the mountains and down the margin of the Hudson in a vast plain, at the present day cut up into highly cultivated farms, and diversified by little eminences, groves, and one large tract of swamp-land. Along the southern margin of the creek the hill forms a lofty and picturesque bank, in some places dropping to the water in a sheer descent of forty or fifty feet, and in others, sloping down in a more gradual but still abrupt fall, broken into little ravines, and thickly covered with a fine growth of young timber.

A foot-path winds up from the stone dwelling, which we have already described, along the upper verge of this bank to the level of the plain, terminating in a singular projection of earth which shoots out from the face of the bank some feet over the stream, taking the form of a huge serpent's head. This projection commands a fine view of the village, and is known to the inhabitants by the title of "Hoppy Nose," from a tradition attached to it. The foot-path, which terminates at this point, receives a melancholy interest from the constant presence of a singular being who has trod it regularly for years. Hour after hour, and day after day, through sunshine and storm, he is to be seen winding among the trees, or moving with a slow monotonous walk along this track, where it verges into the rich sward. Speechless he has been for many years, not from inability, but from a settled, unbroken habit of silence. He is perfectly gentle and inoffensive, and from his quiet bearing a slight observer might mistake him for a meditative philosopher, rather than a man slightly and harmlessly insane as a peculiar expression in his clear, blue eyes and his resolute silence must surely proclaim him to be.

But we are describing subsequent things, rather than the scenery as it existed at the time of our story. Then, the hillside and all the broad plain was a forest of heavy timbered land, but the bank of the creek was much in its present condition. The undergrowth throve a little more luxuriantly, and the "Hoppy Nose" shot out from it covered with a thick coating of grass, but shrubless with the exception of two or three saplings and a few clumps of wild-flowers.

As the moon arose on the night after Sarah Jones' interview with the Indian woman, that singular being stood upon the "Hoppy Nose," waiting the appearance of young Danforth. More than once she went out to the extreme verge of the projection, looked eagerly up and down the stream, then back into the shadow again, with folded arms, continued her watch as before.

At length a slight sound came from the opposite side; she sprang forward, and supporting herself by a sapling, bent over the stream, with one foot just touching the verge of the projection, her lip slightly parted, and her left hand holding back the hair from her temples, eager to ascertain the nature of the sound. The sapling bent and almost snapped beneath her hold, but she remained motionless, her eyes shining in the moonlight with a strange, uncertain luster and keenly fixed on the place whence the sound proceeded.

A canoe cut out into the river, and made toward the spot where she was standing.

"It is he!" broke from her parted lips, as the moonlight fell on the clear forehead and graceful form of a young man who stood upright in the little shallop, and drawing a deep breath, she settled back, folded her arms, and waited his approach.

The sapling had scarcely swayed back to its position, when the youth curved his canoe round to a hollow in the bank and climbing along the ascent, he drew himself up the steep side of the "Hoppy Nose" by the brushwood, and sprang to the Indian woman's side.

"Malaeska," he said, extending his hand with a manner and voice of kindly recognition; "my good, kind nurse, believe me, I am rejoiced to have found you again."

Malaeska did not take his hand, but after an intense and eager gaze into his face, flung herself on his bosom, sobbing aloud, murmuring soft, broken words of endearment, and trembling all over with a rush of unconquerable tenderness.

The youth started back, and a frown gathered on his haughty forehead. His prejudices were offended, and he strove to put her from his bosom; even gratitude for all her goodness could not conquer the disgust with which he recoiled from the embrace of a savage. "Malaeska," he said, almost sternly, attempting to unclasp her arms from his neck, "You forget—I am no longer a boy—be composed, and say what I can do for you?"

But she clung to him the more passionately, and answered with an appeal that thrilled to his very heart.

"Put not your mother away—she has waited long—my son! my son!"

67

The youth did not comprehend the whole meaning of her words. They were more energetic and full of pathos than he had ever witnessed before; but she had been his nurse, and he had been long absent from her, and the strength of her attachment made him for a moment forgetful of her race. He was affected almost to tears.

"Malaeska," he said kindly, "I did not know till now how much you loved me. Yet it is not strange—I can remember when you were almost a mother to me."

"*Almost!*" she exclaimed, throwing back her head till the moonlight revealed her face. "Almost! William Danforth, as surely as there is a God to witness my words, you are my own son!"

The youth started, as if a dagger had been thrust to his heart. He forced the agitated woman from his bosom, and, bending forward, gazed sternly into her eyes.

"Woman, are you mad? Dare you assert this to *me*?"

He grasped her arm almost fiercely, and seemed as if tempted to offer some violence, for the insult her words had conveyed; but she lifted her eyes to his with a look of tenderness, in painful contrast with his almost insane gaze.

"Mad my son?" she said, in a voice that thrilled with a sweet and broken earnestness on the still air. "It was a blessed madness—the madness of two warm young hearts that forgot every thing in the sweet impulse with which they clung together; it was madness which led your father to take the wild Indian girl to his bosom, when in the bloom of early girlhood. Mad! oh, I could go mad with very tenderness, when I think of the time when your little form was first placed in my arms; when my heart ached with love to feel your little hand upon my bosom, and your low murmur fill my ear. Oh, it was a sweet madness. I would die to know it again."

The youth had gradually relaxed his hold on her arm, and stood looking upon her as one in a dream, his arms dropping helplessly as if they had been suddenly paralyzed; but when she again drew toward him, he was aroused to frenzy.

"Great God!" he almost shrieked, dashing his hand against his forehead. "No, no! it can not—I, an Indian? a half-blood? the grandson of my father's murderer? Woman, speak the truth; word for word, give me the accursed history of my disgrace. If I am your son, give me proof—proof, I say!"

When the poor woman saw the furious passion she had raised, she sunk back in silent terror, and it was several minutes before she could answer his wild appeal. When she did speak it was gaspingly and in terror. She told him all—of his birth; his father's death; of her voyage to Manhattan; and of the cruel promise that had been wrung from her, to conceal the relationship between herself and her child. She spoke of her solitary life in the wigwam, of the yearning power which urged her mother's heart to claim the love of her only child, when that child appeared in her neighborhood. She asked not to be acknowledged as his parent, but only to live with him, even as a bond servant, if he willed it.

He stood perfectly still, with his pale face bent to hers, listening to her quick gasping speech, till she had done. Then she could see that his face was convulsed in the moonlight, and that he trembled and grasped a sapling which stood near for support. His voice was that of one utterly overwhelmed and broken-hearted.

"Malaeska," he said, "unsay all this, if you would not see me die at your feet. I am young, and a world of happiness was before me. I was about to be married to one so gentle—so pure—I, an Indian—was about to give my stained hand to a lovely being of untainted blood. I, who was so proud of lifting her to my lofty station. Oh, Malaeska!" he exclaimed, vehemently grasping her hand with a clutch of iron, "say that this was a story—a sad, pitiful story got up to punish my pride? say but this, and I will give you all I have on earth—every farthing. I will love you better than a thousand sons." His frame shook with agitation, and he gazed upon her as one pleading for his life.

When the wretched mother saw the hopeless misery which she had heaped upon her proud and sensitive child, she would have laid down her life could she have unsaid the tale which had wrought such agony, without bringing a stain of falsehood on her soul.

But words are fearful weapons, never to be checked when once put in motion. Like barbed arrows they enter the heart, and can not be withdrawn again, even by the hand that has shot them. The poor Indian mother could not recall hers, but she tried to soothe the proud feelings which had been so terribly wounded.

"Why should my son scorn the race of his mother? The blood which she gave him from her heart was that of a brave and kingly line, warriors and chieftains, all—"

The youth interrupted her with a low bitter laugh. The deep prejudices which had been instilled into his nature—pride, despair, every feeling which urges to madness and evil— were a fire in his heart.

"So I have a patent of nobility to gild my sable birthright, an ancestral line of dusky chiefs to boast of. I should have known this, when I offered my hand to that lovely girl. She little knew the dignity which awaited her union. Father of heaven, my heart will break—I am going mad!"

He looked wildly around as he spoke, and his eyes settled on the dark waters, flowing so tranquilly a few feet beneath him. Instantly he became calm, as one who had found an unexpected resource in his affliction. His face was perfectly colorless and gleamed like marble as he turned to his mother, who stood in a posture of deep humility and supplication a few paces off, for she dared not approach him again either with words of comfort or tenderness. All the sweet hopes which had of date been so warm in her heart, were utterly crushed. She was a heart-broken, wretched woman, without a hope on this side the grave. The young man drew close to her, and taking both her hands, looked sorrowfully into her face. His voice was tranquil and deep-toned, but a slight husky sound gave an unnatural solemnity to his words.

"Malaeska," he said, raising her hands toward heaven, "swear to me by the God whom we both worship, that you have told me nothing but the truth; I would have no doubt."

There was something sublime in his position, and in the solemn calmness which had settled upon him. The poor woman had been weeping, but the tears were checked in her eyes, and her pale lips ceased their quivering motion and became firm, as she looked up to the white face bending over her.

"As I hope to meet you, my son, before that God, I have spoken nothing but the truth."

"Malaeska!"

"Will you not call me mother?" said the meek woman, with touching pathos. "I know I am an Indian, but your father loved me."

"Mother? Yes, God forbid that I should refuse to call you mother; I am afraid that I have often been harsh to you, but I did not know your claim on my love. Even now, I have been unkind."

"No, no, my son."

"I remember you were always meek and forgiving—you forgive me now, my poor mother?"

Malaeska could not speak, but she sank to her son's feet, and covered his hand with tears and kisses.

"There is one who will feel this more deeply than either of us. You will comfort her, Mala—mother will you not?"

Malaeska rose slowly up, and looked into her son's face. She was terrified by his child-like gentleness; her breath came painfully. She knew not why it was, but a shudder ran through her frame, and her heart grew heavy, as if some terrible catastrophe were about to happen. The young man stepped a pace nearer the bank, and stood motionless, gazing down into the water. Malaeska drew close to him, and laid her hand on his arm.

"My son, why do you stand thus? Why gaze so fearfully upon the water?"

He did not answer, but drew her to his bosom, and pressed his lips down upon her forehead. Tears sprang afresh to the mother's eyes, and her heart thrilled with an exquisite sensation, which was almost pain. It was the first time he had kissed her since his childhood. She trembled with mingled awe and tenderness as he released her from his embrace, and put her gently from the brink of the projection. The action had placed her back toward him. She turned—saw him clasp his hands high over his heed, and spring into the air. There was a plunge, the deep rushing sound of waters flowing back to their place, and then a shriek, sharp and full of terrible agony, rung over the stream like the death-cry of a human being.

The cry broke from the wretched mother, as she tore off her outer garments and plunged after the self-murderer. Twice the moonlight fell upon her pallid face and her long hair, as it streamed out on the water. The third time another marble face rose to the surface, and with almost superhuman strength the mother bore up the lifeless body of her son with one arm, and with the other struggled to the shore. She carried him up the steep bank where, at another time, no woman could have clambered even without incumbrance, and laid him on the grass. She tore open his vest, and laid her hand upon the heart. It was cold and pulseless. She chafed his palms, rubbed his marble forehead, and stretching herself on his body, tried to breathe life into his marble lips from her own cold heart. It was in vain. When convinced of this, she ceased all exertion; her face fell forward to the earth, and, with a low sobbing breath, she lay motionless by the dead. The villagers hearing that fearful shriek, rushed down to the stream and reached the "Hoppy Nose", to find two human beings lying upon it.

The next morning found a sorrowful household in Arthur Jones' dwelling. In the "out-room" lay the body of William Danforth, shrouded in his winding-sheet. With her heavy eyes fixed on the marble features of her son, sat the wretched Indian mother. Until the evening before, her dark hair had retained the volume and gloss of youth, but now it fell back from her hollow temples profusely as ever, but perfectly gray. The frost of grief had changed it in a single night. Her features were sunken, and she sat by the dead, motionless and resigned. There was nothing of stubborn grief about her. She answered when spoken to, and was patient in her suffering; but all could see that it was but the tranquility of a broken heart, mild in its utter desolation. When the villagers gathered for the funeral, Malaeska, in a few gentle words, told them of her relationship to the dead, and besought them to bury him by the side of his father.

The coffin was carried out and a solemn train followed it through the forest. Women and children all went forth to the burial.

When the dead body of her affianced husband was brought home, Sarah Jones had been carried senseless to her chamber. She was falling continually from one fainting fit to another, murmuring sorrowfully in her intervals of consciousness, and dropping gently away with the sad words on her lips. Late in the night, after her lover's interment, she awoke to a consciousness of misfortune. As the light dawned, a yearning wish awoke in her heart to visit the grave of her betrothed. She arose, dressed herself, and bent her way with feeble step toward the forest. Strength returned to her as she went forward.

The wigwam was desolate, and the path which led to the grave lay with the dew yet unbroken on its turf. The early sunshine was playing among the wet, heavy branches of the hemlock, when she reached the inclosure. A sweet fragrance was shed over the trampled grass from the white rose-tree which bent low beneath the weight of its pure blossoms. A shower of damp petals lay upon the chieftain's grave, and the green leaves quivered in the air as it sighed through them with a pleasant and cheering motion. But Sarah saw nothing but a newly-made grave, and stretched upon its fresh sods the form of a human being. A feeling of awe came over the maiden's heart. She moved reverently onward, feeling that she was in the sanctuary of the dead. The form was Malaeska's. One arm fell over the grave, and her long hair, in all its mournful change of color, had been swept back from her forehead, and lay tangled amid the rank grass. The sod on which her head rested was sprinkled over with tiny white blossoms. A handful lay crushed beneath her cheek, and sent up a faint odor over the marble face. Sarah bent down and touched the forehead. It was cold and hard, but a tranquil sweetness was there which told that the spirit had passed away without a struggle. Malaeska lay dead among the graves of her household, the heart-broken victim of an unnatural marriage.

CPSIA information can be obtained
at www.ICGtesting.com
Printed in the USA
LVHW010055180722
723719LV00002B/338